R.J. Fitzharris, Wiggy to many, is a science-fiction lover, roleplaying game enthusiast and self-confessed geek. He began writing at the young age of ten, using his grandmother's old typewriter, and has been developing his voice ever since. When not writing, he enjoys seaside walks, good food, and good games with friends and family in his hometown of Plymouth, UK.

To my Grandmother Josephine Jago. You were the one who got me writing in the first place, the reason I am where I am now. All my love and thanks to you, you're a shining star.

And to my granddad, rest soundly until I see you amongst the stars.

R.J. Fitzharris

NO HOPE FROM NOWHERE

AUSTIN MACAULEY PUBLISHERS™

LONDON • CAMBRIDGE • NEW YORK • SHARJAH

A CIP catalogue record for this title is available from the British Library.

ISBN 9781788482394 (Paperback)
ISBN 9781788482400 (Hardback)
ISBN 9781528954280 (ePub e-book)

www.austinmacauley.com

First Published (2019)
Austin Macauley Publishers Ltd
25 Canada Square
Canary Wharf
London
E14 5LQ

Ruth Rees-Williams, my closest friend, you're like family to me. You have encouraged me, told me never to give up, and have always helped me to continue fighting for my dreams. You have stood by me through thick and thin, I couldn't ask for a better friend.

From the bottom of my heart, thank you.

Prologue

In the late 21st century, humanity expanded into the stars. Many people believed it was just the next logical step in the advancement of our race, but others knew the truth. We did not so much expand into the stars as flee into them. Running away from our own hubris and a world left to rot at the hands of our own reckless desires. Earth became a foot note in the history of humanity, something to tell the grandchildren over dinner.

At first we built monumental colonies on other planets in our home system. From the scientific institutions of Mars, the floating habitats of Venus and the solar farms of Mercury to the under-ice military facilities on Europa or the aptly named 'Gateway to Nowhere' on Pluto, we made every effort to remain close to home. Yet it was never enough for those who sought to truly conquer the stars and so the Stellar-Traveller project was born.

Trillions of System Dollars were poured into making the Stellar-Traveller project a reality. Sixteen state of the art vessels, dubbed arks, filled with ten thousand ambitious souls seeking a new life in systems far beyond known space. It was an ambitious project, but not too ambitious for the power hungry corporations and national governments who wanted their first piece of *'Nowhere'*.

They would cryogenically freeze all but a thousand of the Stellar-Traveller participants. Those thousand volunteers would live out their lives, the lives of their children, grandchildren and possibly great grandchildren amongst the stars, keeping the arks flying to their destination. The destination, or *'Nowhere'*, was different for each participating vessel with the hope of bringing humanity to a vast array of systems and building a lasting legacy for a race running out of home space into which they could expand.

With no idea of what would await them, the Stellar-Travellers launched themselves head first into the unknown. Falling asleep to awaken hundreds or thousands of years later, not knowing what they would face. Many of the vessels were lost within decades of leaving, most through galactic phenomena, others simply disappeared. Only five were known to have successfully reached their destination, the most prominent of which would go on to become the pinnacle of human pioneer spirit. There a new systems alliance was born, the heart of a new frontier and the shining light for the future of mankind. But amongst this new world, one of humanity's greatest flaws still festered.

War was inevitable.

Chapter One

Nobody remembers why it started. Even the studious, often all knowing, scholar Nishfar Montiz could only recall the effects of that first night; the night the sky turned red. Years past, his grandparents had been on the first colony ship to reach Hakon IV and it was the only planet he had ever truly known. They told him stories of their native system, and the planet Earth from where humanity had travelled. But to humanity, Earth was now little more than a forgotten dream; an embellished story told to children to make them proud of their heritage.

On that first night, alone in his study, Nishfar had stared at the night sky as he did most evenings, contemplating the future of humanity. With a dusty, broken yet well bound tome called 'Contingency Ships: Fact or Fiction' open and upside down upon his lap, he tapped his fingers and hummed the tune of Mars; his favourite orchestral piece. He witnessed the first streaks of light, the fires that broke the atmosphere. Mere seconds later the sky turned red and Nishfar stopped humming, overcome with equal parts curiosity and fear. Soon after, the ground began to shake, the windows began to rattle and all around him his world began to rumble. Multiple explosions rocked the horizon, sending huge plumes of fire and smoke rising towards the stars. Nishfar's windows exploded inward with the first blast, covering him in glass. Sheer force took the wind out of Nishfar, causing him to gasp for a much needed breath, only just managing to remain conscious. He would never forget this night, the night the sky turned red, the night the war began.

As the dust settled following the first wave of attacks, semi-orbital strikes Nishfar knew were to unsettle and destroy Hakon IV's will to fight, the scholar pulled himself to his feet. His study, his entire house, was a mess. Staring out into the now illuminated night, ablaze with the fires that burned across the colony Nishfar was frozen by shock. Where previously a calm silence had covered the land, now the sounds of roaring flame, the screams of panicked citizens and the sirens of emergency vehicles echoed all around.

Despite living on the outskirts of the colony, at the edge of the continental rainforest, Nishfar found himself dreadfully close to conflict. His neighbours, although they were few, had already ventured out onto the street. Their expressions a mixture of surprise, worry and fear as they stood in their night wear and dressing gowns. Steadily a rumble began to grow, a reverberation that started off akin to a stampede but soon grew to resemble that of fusion powered atmospheric craft. Nishfar, and his neighbours, looked all about them yet could see nothing; then Nishfar was struck by cold realisation. Fear frozen in his expression he ran onto his lawn yelling, calling to his neighbours to move, to seek cover, but it was too late. The bombers appeared over the tree line and in seconds, lit up the street and the houses beyond. Nishfar watched as his neighbours, men, women and children, were gunned down, blown apart or burned to a crisp by the hideous firepower laid upon them. So close was the assault that Nishfar found himself blown clean off his feet, back onto his porch, sliding backwards into his doorway.

Dazed, and confused, Nishfar tried to pull himself to his feet. All around him the fires burned, his own home succumbing to the blinding heat as the flames devoured all within their path. He watched as a man stumbled out of the flames, a neighbour, someone he had known for nearly five years. His skin was melting, his dying screams hauntingly stentorian and Nishfar was powerless to help him. The scholar watched in horror as his neighbour collapsed into a crawl at the end of the lawn, his screams finally silenced when the sweet release of death took him.

***

Nishfar awoke with a cry, "No!!!" he cried out, sweat dripping from his brow, his breathing heavy. Layla Montiz, his wife, pressed her hand against his chest.

"Neesh, Neesh it's OK," she whispered, placing her lips to his cheek with a loving tenderness. "You're safe. It's OK." Nishfar's staggered breathing continued, his eyes darting about the room as his mind struggled to emerge from the dream. "It's OK, it's OK," Layla continued. "You're safe, we're safe." It had been six months since the colonial war began, since the night the sky turned red. Every attempt at sleep since, Nishfar's dreams were plagued by the horrors he had witnessed on that night and the death of the neighbour before his eyes.

The city of New Pavonis, his home, had been destroyed that night. Nishfar was one of less than three thousand survivors, a quarter of the total population. Displaced, like thousands of other civilians, he was overlooked by New Pavonis' very own defenders and the enemy that sought to bring the colony down. Once war had come, forces on both sides cared little for the collateral damage and the casualties of their wanton destruction; victory, it seemed, was their only goal. Nishfar had witnessed it first-hand. Thankfully his wife Layla, and their seven year old daughter Mahira, had been with her parents in New Peraea, one hundred and forty five miles due north of New Pavonis. It was a fact he was grateful for every day since, for where others had lost their families he still had his.

"I'm sorry," he huffed. "The fires, the bombs, they…"

"I know Neesh, I know. But we're safe here, we're safe with my parents," Layla whispered, tracing her hand across his chest and then wiping his brow, tucking his short curled locks behind his ear. Nishfar looked into his wife's eyes with a smile, cradling her head in his hand and tracing his thumb across her lips.

"I'll be OK," he whispered back, his breath finally returning to him. "In time I'll be OK." He turned his attention towards his chest and his pyjama trousers, both drenched in sweat. Turning back to Layla he smiled and kissed her on the forehead. "I think I'll grab a quick shower."

"OK," she responded, gazing lovingly into his eyes.

As he rolled out of bed and placed his feet into his slippers, she looked at him with a mixture of love and concern. She knew her husband had been deeply affected by that first night, even to her he had barely spoken of the horrors he had witnessed. Layla wished nothing more than to once again be with the man she married but before her stood a stained canvas, a dulled reflection of that same man.

Wiping the steam from the bathroom mirror, the shower running behind him, Nishfar stared deep into his own wearied eyes. His face was weathered by six months of insomnia and stress, his eyes forlorn and his beard dishevelled. Turning on the cold tap and cupping his hands underneath, he caught the cold water and splashed it on his face.

"You couldn't help them," he whispered to himself, "the fires were too much." Suddenly the bathroom shook. The pot of toothbrushes smashed to the tile floor along with many of the accessories. Nishfar quickly grabbed the mirror to stop it from toppling as the shower behind him spluttered to a stop. A brief few seconds of silence followed before a massive boom shook the room again.

Nishfar darted into the hallway where Layla now stood, staring out of their bedroom door with fear in her eyes. At the far end of the hall Layla's parents, aged and frail, stood in their dressing gowns, their own eyes filled with a mixture of fear and confusion. Another tremor shook the building again, Layla's mother lost her footing and fell to the ground. As her father dropped to his knee's to help his wife up Layla crossed the hallway toward them. With the same pattern as the first a few seconds of silence followed before another massive explosion. Windows shattering accompanied the most recent blast, the sounds of glass and shrapnel colliding with walls and furniture reverberating throughout the house.

"Mahira!" Layla shouted toward Nishfar, but he was already darting across the hallway towards their daughter's room. With little care for the handle he burst through the door with his shoulder, the impact causing a sharp pain easily ignored as the adrenaline surged through him. Mahira's bed was covered in glass, a strong breeze filtering into the room as her street facing window had imploded. Nishfar looked frantically around the room yet he could not see his daughter.

"Mahira!!!" he called out. Layla popped her head through the door as well,

"Mahira, sweetie!!!" she also called but there was no answer. The house shook again.

"GET DOWN!" Nishfar shouted, grabbing Layla and diving to the ground, putting the bed between them and the window. As he predicted a few seconds passed and then, like clockwork, a huge boom louder than before shook their surroundings. A huge gust of air filled the room with dust, the orange glow of fire

14

brightening the darkness beyond. An eerie silence followed yet not for Nishfar, he could make out a weeping from behind him. He pulled the duvet up revealing the underneath of the bed and both parents looked under. Clutching her favourite teddy, 'Ikle Paulie' as she called him, Mahira stared back at them.

"Daddy?" she called out, a faint yet unassured smile crossing her lips.

"Mahira darling, stars be praised! I am happy to see you," he said, a tear in his eye. She crawled out and into his arms, Layla grabbing them both as well. Soon enough, the house shook once more. "We need to get under the stairs," Nishfar said, his words tinged with despair, "they're here."

Layla helped her parents down the stairs as another explosion shook the house, forcing them to the ground. Behind them Nishfar stood with Mahira in his arms, sweat once again pouring from his brow. As the building shook around him he steeled himself, planted like a strong oak. "Quickly," he called to Layla. "The explosions are getting closer." He could see the fear in the eyes of each member of his family and yet he was powerless to ease it. They had not experienced the cruel hand of war as he had, not until now. Here they were potentially about to face the very same horrors he had witnessed not six months ago. Nishfar knew he had to stay strong, to not show weakness. This was not a show of masculinity but a stoic, fatherly strength for his Mahira. She had just seen her window blown inwards, seen her parents dive for cover and witnessed her room illuminated by the fires of war. She had been left sobbing in her father's arms and he knew he had to stay strong for her. However there was also something else he needed to do for himself and his own sense of redemption.

As the family all huddled into the cupboard under the stairs, a single fusion bulb for light, Nishfar looked at his wife and immediately she knew he intended to do something other than remain. Layla shook her head, her expression pleading with him not to, but deep down she knew he would not listen. Nishfar kissed his little girl on the forehead, held both her and Layla tight then stepped out, closing the door behind him.

"Where is Daddy going?" Mahira whimpered.

"To make sure other people are safe like us," Layla responded, a tear in her eye. "That's not Daddy's job!" Mahira continued, holding 'Ikle Paulie' tight to her chest. "I know sweetie, I know."

***

The heat was inconceivable, the air near thick with smoke. Nishfar could barely breathe as he stepped outside. He slammed the keypad for the front door, forcing it shut behind him. Several barely audible beeps notified him that the door was locked and the security system was enabled. For now his in-law's home was secure. Their road was on the fifth tier of the Soleri Arcology, which formed the centre of New Peraea. It was a phenomenal structure originally built on Earth and launched at the dawn of colonial space travel; it was the first major structure of its kind and the initial settlement upon colonisation of Hakon IV. The Arcology was not only home to nearly one million affluent citizens, of which Nishfar's in-laws were a pair of the more well-to-do, but it was also home to the planetary government. Housed in the Grand Apex Hall, at the peak of the Arcology, towering more than four thousand five hundred feet above sea level, were congress and the office of the Madame President. With an entirely steel-glass surround it was the epitome of human architecture that provided beautiful surroundings within which to conduct political debate.

Nishfar stumbled across the road to the four inch thick, meter high, sapphire glass window that separated the road from the void in the centre of the Arcology. Cries of countless residents echoed all around, equal parts surprised, shocked and frightened. Nearly two hundred and eighty feet opposite, across the void at the centre of the Arcology, the entire west wing was ablaze. A gaping hole torn straight through. Nishfar helplessly looked on as he witnessed citizens flinging themselves into the void, facing certain death just to escape the flames. Like six months before, he was forced to watch and listen as people cried for help they would never receive. The Arcology's fire defence systems had kicked in, several AI operated drones flying into action yet their attempts to combat the inferno were futile. As Nishfar stared blankly at the suffering another explosion rocked the Arcology. A bright flash blinded him, shattering the sapphire glass and hurling him across the road like a rag doll. He collided with the wall, knocking him for six and ripping the wind from his lungs.

Dazed and confused, Nishfar struggled to pull himself to his feet and reassess his surroundings. Sirens blared as a six wheeled police enforcement vehicle skidded to a stop near him. The side windows switched from blacked out to clear and a single officer stared out from the driver's seat. "Sir, please get inside!" the officer commanded, his voice broadcast through the six wheelers external speakers. He showed little politeness and it was clear he was as unnerved as Nishfar, his face betraying as much.

"Those people need all the help they can get. I'm here to help!" Nishfar insisted, his tone pleading.

"This is not a request. Please return to your abode!" the officer continued. Nishfar intended to dispute the request further but a flash of light and wave of heat overcame him.

The scholar raised his hand to cover his face and instinctively crouched to his knees, a choice that would prove fortuitous. Erupting into flame, the six wheeler exploded, immediately followed by the electronic hiss of gun fire. Nishfar wasn't familiar with all types of firearm, but he was familiar with a few and he was certain that the ones he could hear were military grade. But they weren't standard issue for Hakon IV Forces, those he'd witnessed used during the night the sky turned red. These were railguns; expensive, outlawed weapons used by no mainstream force of his knowledge; yet here they were.

The whistle of projectiles, and the near kiss of death they brought with them, was enough to force Nishfar to take further cover behind the six wheelers burning husk. The officer inside had been immolated leaving barely a skeleton, frozen in a pose he had been in mere seconds previous. The disgruntled scholar did his best to ignore it, putting it to the back of his mind as his attention was drawn by screams from along the road. Peering out from behind the wreckage, careful not to fully reveal his position, he bore witness to further horrors. A squad of ten heavily armoured metallic warriors, painted as black as shadow, fired indiscriminately on any man, woman or child. These invaders bore no insignia nor flag to identify them as members of a particular colony or group. Much to his consternation, Nishfar looked on as four of the same squad fired unreservedly on civilians. A defenceless man, his husband, and their children were torn down without a care whilst another couple were gunned down in an equally indiscriminate fashion, scrambling for the supposed safety of their car. Towards the centre of the cluster a single member of the terrifying unit raised one of his huge metallic arms. A gauntlet of large, clamp like fingers, with sharpened edges that glinted in the fluorescent light, pointed in Nishfar's direction. That armoured figure motioned for the squad to head for him. With military precision, they did so.

Nishfar froze with fear, slamming himself against the burning wreck and grunting as the heat burned his skin. With each step the squad took the ground rumbled, his heart racing harder the closer they drew. Nishfar's heart began to sink, resigned to his own demise, then the door to his in-laws house opened. Time seemed to slow to a perceptible crawl, his expression darkening as he looked on to find Layla staring at him with a mixture of relief and surprise. He shook his head, frantically gesturing his hand for her to take a step back but Layla didn't understand. The electrical charge and subsequent hiss of rail-gunfire broke through the roar of the flames and the screams of their neighbours. Nishfar watched in horror, sorrow gripping his already battered heart as Layla's chest exploded with a single mortal shot. Her eyes frozen by the biting kiss of death. "Noooooooooooo!!!" Nishfar yelled out, his voice breaking with vehement sorrow.

***

The force of the hit had taken her clean off her feet, throwing her to the floor. Blood started to saturate her night dress as she gasped for air, shock griping her broken body. With no thought for his own safety, Nishfar leapt to his feet, ran across the road and dived through the door. He felt a shot graze his leg and another, his thigh, but his adrenaline was pumping to the point he didn't care for the damage or pain. Hitting the ground with a thud, he took no time to gather himself before leaping up and striking the emergency lock. Alarms blared as the security shutters slammed down all around him and a pre-programmed electronic voice informed him security personnel would be on site momentarily. Rail-gunfire collided with the reinforced steel of the security door, the familiar plink echoing throughout the hallway. Cradling his wife in his arms, Nishfar sobbed. Her breathing was broken and her eyes frozen in time, so gravely wounded that she could hardly muster her words. At that moment the tears began to stream uncontrollably from Nishfar's eyes as he wrestled with a nearby coat in a futile attempt to staunch her bleeding.

"I...love..." Layla attempted to speak, but she couldn't muster the strength to complete her sentence.

"I know. I know. I love you too," Nishfar cried, tears running into his mouth and being spat out with the force of his words. Coughing and spluttering he struggled to breathe through his crippling sorrow. In his arms he cradled his wife, the woman he had known for nearly twenty years, the love of his life, his world and now she was gone. "No! Not you... Not here... Not like this!" he coughed, holding her tightly, rocking back and forth. The railgun fire on the door intensified, but Nishfar cared little, he was a beaten and broken man.

Ten minutes passed. Nishfar's expression painted a portrait of a man oppressed by loss, withered and aged by heartache. Mucus poured from his nose mixing with his tears, but he didn't even attempt to wipe it away. Instead he just held Layla tighter and tighter to his chest. The gun fire had stopped, though Nishfar hadn't noticed. There had not been an explosion in nearly twenty minutes, still he did not notice. There he just sat in the hallway, in a pool of his wife's blood, clutching on to her lifeless body.

The sound of the under-stair cupboard opening broke the silence.

"DON'T COME OUT," Nishfar spat, his words commanding, yet broken. "Not yet, not now."

"We heard gunfire," Layla's father explained, stepping out against Nishfar's request. The old congressman froze as he laid eyes upon his daughter's lifeless body. Unable to muster any words he waved for his wife to stay back, knowing she held Mahira tightly in her arms. He struggled to hold back his tears, doing so only long enough so that his granddaughter would not see. Closing the door behind him he walked forwards slowly. His eyes were filled with a forlorn hope, a wish that what he bore witness to was not the truth. Nishfar remained sobbing uncontrollably, still clenching Layla tightly, rocking her back and forth. Her father stepped forwards, placing a reassuring hand upon his shoulder. As the congressman gripped Nishfar's shoulders tightly, his emotion seemed to flow through his grasp. "It's not your fault," he whispered, holding back the overwhelming pain of his broken heart. "Don't you dare think this is your fault."

"I couldn't save them. I couldn't save *her*," Nishfar responded with a whimper.

The door to the cupboard under the stairs opened with a familiar whoosh. Nishfar stood silhouetted by the fluorescent light of the hallway, clearly broken but without tears, his expression doing well to maintain a strong facade. His dark pyjama trousers hid the blood in which they were drenched and he had wiped all traces from his bare torso. His mother-in-law looked at him with eyes that spoke a thousand words. She knew what had transpired but she wouldn't show in front of her granddaughter. Mahira looked to her father with her innocent smile and pale green eyes, that coupled with the way she clenched 'Ikle Paulie' calmed Nishfar. His daughter's innocence brought a much needed smile to his lips, but with it the tears soon returned.

"Daddy, where did Mummy go?" she questioned, reaching out for him. He stepped into the cupboard and grabbed her in his arms, holding her close, tighter than he had done for a long time.

He was broken and now he had to do something every father dreaded, he had to break his own daughter's heart.

"Mummy… Mummy had to go away… To the stars," he wept.

"Why didn't she say goodbye?" Mahira cried, breaking down in her father's arms. Looking at his daughter, Nishfar struggled to remain as stoic as possible.

"Mummy wanted to say goodbye… She really did," he whispered, his speech cracking under the weight of his grief. "But she had to go quickly. The stars called her home." Mahira wept uncontrollably with her father. Nishfar was no longer strong enough to hold back the full extent of his sorrow and together they cried.

"I wanted to say goodbye, Daddy," she whimpered, misery breaking her speech.

"I know sweetheart… So did I."

Chapter Two

Nishfar traced his finger around the rim of the ornate, porcelain tea cup before him. He sat overlooking the grand rainforests beneath the Arcology from the comfort of his in-law's balcony. It was a beautiful day, the three suns shining a warming light upon the enormous self-contained city. The air was crisp, not too hot and yet equally not too cold. All around him the faint sound of construction echoed across the Arcology as New Peraea made haste with its repairs. Two weeks of battle had left it battered, bruised and yet not broken; which was more than could be said for Nishfar.

Staring up at the two majestic battle cruisers that floated high above, Nishfar's mind drifted to the memory of his wife. He could see on the horizon, nearly three miles out, the all too familiar signs of war. Smoke billowing in the air, atmospheric war machines darting back and forth followed by the occasional explosive flash of light that no doubt signalled the death of countless souls; souls not unlike his wife. His mind was plagued by 'what ifs' and 'could haves', but in every instance the scholar could not see a way in which he could have rescued Layla from what was. She was gone and no matter how hard he tried, he could not escape the near crippling feeling that he was responsible.

A smooth electronic whoosh shook him from his contemplation as the balcony door opened. Layla's father walked out, dressed in the ceremonial garb of the planetary congress. The President had made a Quorum call, wishing all congressmen to be present in order to pass critical legislation to aid with the war. Hakon IV and its various settlements were still in shock. Many of the settlements had already fallen, starting with New Pavonis on the night the sky turned red. Although the major news broadcasts wouldn't say as much, Nishfar knew that the planet was losing the war, and today's Quorum call proved that the Madam President was feeling the strain.

"So what happened Congressman?" Nishfar questioned, refusing to turn to acknowledge Layla's father. "Are we about to take more lives, like the wars of Earth, the ones nobody talks about?"

"Nishfar, you've known me long enough, call me Daav'id," Layla's father responded, taking a seat at the table and reaching to pour himself a warm cup of tea. "It's what Layla would have wanted." Nishfar's head dropped, his chin near touching his chest as a faint smile crossed his lips. Peace followed as Daav'id sipped at his tea and awaited his son-in-law's response. Nishfar continued to trace his finger around the rim of his cup, having been doing so for the last hour.

"You're right," he whispered with a thoughtful chuckle. "She always told me to stop calling you sir, or congressman. I never listened," he paused, "until now."

"I know, and I never pushed the matter despite her asking me to," Daav'id responded. The pair shared a respectful titter. Nishfar then sighed, "If only she could see us now."

"She'd be happy," Daav'id responded with a smile.

The pair stared out at the conflict in the distance. The three suns were high in the sky, just reaching their zenith and one of the cruisers had moved to a point that shaded the balcony.

"So what happened Daav'id?" Nishfar questioned again, finally taking a sip of his now cold tea.

"Congress and the President have agreed a motion to use increasing force to defend the remaining settlements. Meanwhile an emissary has been sent to the Systems Alliance to request assistance, and to see if we can identify this enemy," Daav'id responded with a shrug. "Current intelligence suggests it's not a group from within our own system, and the intelligence committee and naval intelligence have no further information."

"So, supposedly, the enemy is from beyond our borders?" Nishfar inquisitively questioned. "Are they human?"

Daav'id chuckled, a reaction Nishfar couldn't fathom.

"They are most certainly human. Naval Intelligence has ascertained this much. Extraterrestrial presences have never been noted since the dawn of colonial space travel. You know that," the congressmen posited, "you're the scholar."

"It doesn't mean it could not, or will not, happen," Nishfar responded with a serious demeanour.

"Fair counter, I concede," Daav'id acknowledged.

"So the war shows no signs of leaving this humble planet then?" Nishfar questioned rhetorically. Daav'id sighed and nodded in protracted agreement.

"I need to get Mahira out then," Nishfar continued, looking to his father-in-law for agreement, "I need to put a safe distance between the war and my daughter, if not for her then for Layla." Daav'id shook his head, a melancholic expression overcoming his already placid face. Nishfar looked at him with an inquisitive gaze. The old congressmen turned his head towards Nishfar and stared deep into his eyes.

"The President also passed a motion to lock down the planet. There are no longer any civilian craft permitted to enter or exit Hakon IV's atmosphere, even non-essential government and military vehicles are under strict guidelines", Daav'id lamented. "We are here for the foreseeable future." Nishfar's expression darkened, a rage he didn't know he had filling his expression. Daav'id looked at him with assiduous eyes.

"I'm going to get my daughter out, by whatever means necessary. Do you understand me?" Nishfar growled. "I will protect her, she is all I have."

***

The balcony door slid shut behind Nishfar as he left his father-in-law drinking tea and contemplating the scholar's words. All around him the world seemed cold, empty. Mahira and her grandmother had gone to the Garden District to feed the birds as they often did, they all agreed it would be good for the little girl. She had not spoken to anyone since her mother's funeral, having only said, *"I will miss you Mummy,"* when they scattered the ashes into the wind. Nishfar had hoped that some quality time in the company of her grandmother might change that; he had prayed to the stars that it would.

He trudged through the hallway towards the living room. As he had done every day since the incident, he found himself pausing at the front door, at the very place where Layla had died. He gazed despondently at the empty space. Refreshed with a new carpet and different coloured walls it bore no resemblance to that fateful night and yet, for Nishfar, the memory was still very real. He closed his eyes tightly, diverting them long enough to step into the living room. The electronic door closed behind him automatically and all about him the room burst into life. Within the walls retractable settees emerged, suitably cleaned and re-inflated for comfort, a fireplace arose from the ground at the centre of the room, not yet lit but ready for a simple spoken command to ignite and the lights provided suitable illumination. "Holovid!" Nishfar commanded, as he slumped onto the settee behind him, as exhausted as he had been these past few weeks. A holographic display, near three meters in diameter, burst to life above the fireplace. "Fire set: eighteen degrees. Holovid set: channel ten sixty," he continued, folding his arms.

At speed, flying low across the native rainforests, a news drone made haste northward towards the conflict zone. The holovid broadcast the images with a vivid realism that made one feel like they were truly there. "Enemy forces besieging New Arsia have met staunch resistance by Militia Fighters of the Free Hakon Army," the inhuman, electrical, murmur of an AI news reporter spoke. "The F.H.A. have ignored repeated requests by President Roimata Aroha to stand down and let government forces intercede. Because of this, the military forces of Hakon IV are unable to intervene at this stage. President Aroha has stressed she will not stand by for much longer." The drone reached the outskirts of New Arsia and slowed to a more reasonable pace, taking a sharp left and entering a circle pattern.

The settlement had been torn apart by war. Several of the steel Hab-Blocks were either entirely ablaze, torn asunder or mere shrapnel now scattered throughout the streets. Dropping down into one such street, the drone switched into bipedal mode, its wings transforming into legs. It ducked into cover behind one of the barely standing steel girders that once held together a Hab-Block of multiple levels. "We have come to speak directly to F.H.A. forces to ascertain why they fight the way they fight, and why they ignore the President's repeated requests," the AI reporter continued, its electronic voice conveying zero emotion.

Nishfar looked toward the holovid inquisitively. The Free Hakon Army had been underground for decades. The organisation was supposedly no more than a bunch of glory seeking iconoclasts and radicals who shared a vision of a Hakon IV without government. Although classed as a terrorist organisation, thanks to the words of President Aroha, they had never been dissident nor violent; until now. Nishfar had never been one to believe propaganda, and certainly not the words of individuals in power, but now they were showing signs that they were exactly as President Aroha had described them.

"I'm here at the frontline, in a temporary bunker created by the hard work of the F.H.A.," the AI news reporter continued as the drone walked down a staircase. A fusion light switched on, illuminating the path in front of the drone as it walked through enclosed corridors, some of which were barely wide enough to fit the robotic biped. "These corridors allow the F.H.A. to move freely beneath New Arsia, our sources say that these tunnels cover the entire settlement," the AI posited as it reached an opening, illuminated by archaic light bulbs atop an ancient, rusted generator. As the drone's camera surveyed it with a feigned sense of curiosity the generators roar cancelled out the sounds of battle coming from the surface. "As you can see here, the F.H.A. is not blessed by the resources of our government and instead rely on artefacts from a bygone age, raided from museums or smuggled from off world," the reporter continued. At that point, a large clank echoed and the camera shook.

"State your business, drone!" a grizzled voice called out.

"I am here on behalf of Planetary News First. I'm expected," the AI spoke, slowly turning around. Standing before the drone, aiming a similarly archaic firearm, was a man dressed all in black. With a mask covering his face, black fatigues and a combat vest, he looked nothing like the radicals that the F.H.A. had been painted as in previous newscasts. He looked like one of Hakon IV's own marines.

"You were expected," the soldier commanded, "but the President has alienated us for the last time. We denounce her restriction on interplanetary travel. We denounce her belated use of force. If she won't protect Hakon IV, we will." Before the AI News Reporter could respond the soldier opened fire. The visual feed was broken, the holovid went blank and then the standard apology filled the visual. Nishfar sat upright in shock, he knew that voice. It was Keifar, his brother.

***

Nishfar remembered the day his father last spoke of his brother. *Rain collided violently with the sapphire glass windscreen of his airspeed hatchback. His father, Rin Montiz, stared out across the tarmac with lugubrious eyes. The military base was alive with fervent activity. In the passenger seat Nishfar had looked to his father expectantly. It was near midnight and the pair had been sat in the car, on the tarmac, for nearly three hours. Nishfar had not known why his father had summoned him, or why they had stayed there for so long without speaking. All he knew was that his father had important news, a revelation he couldn't make over communicator. So Nishfar had travelled on foot to New Pavonis Marine Headquarters where his brother had been stationed, to meet his father in the dead of night, for no discernible reason. After three hours of near silence Rin turned to his son and spoke the words Nishfar would never forget: "Your brother was killed in action... I'm here to identify his body."*

That night after his father spoke those fateful words, the pair had exited his vehicle and walked through the torrential rain towards the medical facility. Both were morose, confronting feelings they had hoped they'd never have to. Keifar had always been the hero of the family; where Nishfar had the intellect, Keifar had the strength. Nishfar had hoped that the body they were about to identify was not his brother, but his gut was telling him it was. Rin on the other hand was adamant it was not his son, refusing to accept any scenario in which he was about to find his eldest on a slab.

When the pair entered the medical facility, and the doctor greeted them with an understanding yet regretful expression, it finally began to dawn on the old man that the scenario he would not face may indeed be true. "Mr Montiz. Please follow me, the body of the deceased is right this way," the doctor had said, his tone compassionate.

"Very well," Rin had responded disconsolately.

It was a scene Nishfar remembered with a vivid clarity. He recalled the forlorn trudge of a broken man as he walked behind his father, towards the room in which his brother supposedly lay. A walk that should only have taken a few minutes seemed to last

26

an eternity, although Nishfar suspected a trick of his memory. When they reached the room Rin had turned to Nishfar and forbid him from entering. Moments later he exited, tears streaming from a stone cold expression. The old man had not said a word but Nishfar knew that what he had seen had been a truth he wished not to accept.

To this day Nishfar had believed that his father identified his brother in that room. Rin went on to plan his son's memorial and funeral alone, refusing support from anyone. Whenever Nishfar questioned his father on the condition of his brother, he was shut down. If he challenged his father as to why he wasn't allowed to see his own brother's body, he was spun a noble tale of how he shouldn't have had to see his elder sibling in such a way. Nishfar always believed it was his father's grief that made him so irritable, so defensive. But after last night's news he suddenly hit the realisation that his father's grief was in truth a facade. That the body his father had seen that night at the Marine Headquarters was not his brother's but some stranger's, that for four years Rin had let his entire family believe his son, Nishfar's older brother, Mahira's uncle, was dead.

At the realisation he had been lied to, Nishfar ran into the bathroom and yelled with rage; slamming his fist into the bathroom mirror and shattering it under the force. "All this time you were alive and you didn't get in touch!" he whispered, his words gruff and filled with venom. "You allowed Dad to become complicit in your deceit."

"You OK in there Nishfar?" Layla's mother questioned from outside the door.

"Yes…sorry… I had an accident with the mirror. I'll repair it tomorrow," he responded, trying to mask his fury. "I've just had a tough few months. I apologise, ma'am."

"You don't need to apologise. Venting is good, you should allow yourself to more often. Just preferably not against my home furnishings," she responded with a warm tone, "also if you're going to call Daav'id by his name you must call me Marie, Ma'am is far too formal." Her words brought a much needed smile to his face although his anger still burned deep.

"OK Marie, thank you," he responded with respect.

Staring at his bloodied knuckles and then back to his face, within the broken mirror, Nishfar began to weep uncontrollably. All the pain, loss and deceit of recent weeks had brought him to breaking point. He knew not how he was going to get his daughter to safety, or how to confront his father about the truth of Keifar, or even if he would ever speak to his brother again. Whereas before he would have confided in Layla and she would have given him a sense of direction he now found himself lost. Her parents had given him and Mahira a home where they did not have one. Daav'id had stood by them financially despite the loss of his daughter. The congressman had even motioned for them to gain permanent residence within the Soleri Arcology, residence usually only reserved for the wealthy, government officials and high ranking military personnel. But all this was still not enough, and did little to ease the stress the scholar now faced. He wished he could just be back at the University of New Pavonis, before the night the sky turned red, when he lectured in Colonial History; a simpler time. But deep down, he knew that time had passed. Now Nishfar needed to steel himself for the trials ahead, if not for himself then for Mahira.

The subtle clarinet concerto, the faint melody of strings and the echo of piano keys filled the room as Nishfar slid Mahira's door open. Since her mother had passed the little girl had struggled to sleep, even with the warm embrace of 'Ikle Paulie'. Her grandmother had recommended classical pieces that she herself had written, beautiful compositions that gently kissed the ears and touched the soul. Mahira found it much easier to drift off with her grandmother's music playing than she had done before she listened to it. Daav'id had his maintenance AI install a new music system in her room so that she may hear the sounds of the orchestra from all around her. It created a truly relaxing and pleasant space.

Nishfar was careful not to close the door with much force, less he disturb his daughter. She fidgeted as she realised he had entered, attempting to masquerade as sleeping when in truth she was very much awake. Mahira had heard her father's outburst in the bathroom, and her grandmother's subsequent words to him. She knew he was hurting as much as she was, but as a child she simply didn't know how to express it or how to help him. Nishfar perched himself on the edge of the bed and lightly tucked her hair behind her ear. The corner of her mouth peaked, giving way to a slight smile, although she tried hastily to hide it again. "Mahira my sweet," Nishfar whispered, "Daddy is here."

"Hi Daddy…don't forget 'Ikle Paulie'," she responded with equal reticence, the first words she had said in weeks.

"Oh, I am sorry," Nishfar continued with a welcome smile. "Hello Ikle Paulie, I apologise for not greeting you immediately."

Mahira chuckled, turning over to look up at her father, clenching Ikle Paulie tightly. Nishfar looked at his daughter with nothing but adoration.

"Are you OK Daddy? You're not still sad are you?" Mahira questioned. "If you are then give Ikle Paulie a hug, he's great at hugs."

Nishfar smiled, snuggling down beside his daughter in bed and taking Ikle Paulie in his arms. "You know what would make this hug better?" he questioned.

"If I joined in?" She smiled, to which Nishfar could only nod with an expression of love. It was the kind of love only a father could show his daughter, the sort that spoke a million words and yet said none. The pair hugged closely, Mahira burying her head in her father's chest and grabbing both he and Ikle Paulie tightly.

"I miss Mummy," she whispered, a tear rolling down her cheek.

"I do too sweetie, I do too." Nishfar responded, he too beginning to well up. "But do you know what?"

"What?" she responded with a calm excitement.

"Mummy is watching down on us right now, from the stars, from her new home, and she is wishing she could be here right now to hold us, to hug us tight and to thank 'Ikle Paulie' for looking after her little girl," Nishfar said, a smile on his lips as tears formed in his eyes. "But no matter how far away she is, she loves you with all of her heart and will always protect you."

"I wish I could see her again," Mahira whimpered.

"One day, in the far far far far future, you will my sweetheart, you will. But until then just know that Mummy watches you and she misses you every bit as much as you miss her," Nishfar responded, cuddling her tightly in his arms.

Nishfar's eyes opened and he realised he had drifted off in Mahira's bed, his daughter closely resting on his chest. He took a second to absorb the moment, to accept the peace, before slowly removing himself with a practiced skill perfected through many years of fatherhood. Laying her head gently on the pillow as he stood up, he placed Ikle Paulie in her arms, pulled up her duvet and lightly kissed her forehead. "Cease Music," he whispered, the relaxing sounds of the orchestra fading into silence. "Mahira," he said softly, "Daddy has to go away for a few days. But I promise you I will return. I have to find a way for us to be safe, and to do that I have to go somewhere dangerous first. Because of that I can't risk taking you with me." He slowly stepped backwards towards the door and opened it delicately.

"I love you," he whispered as he stepped out, sliding the door quietly shut behind him.

"I love you too Daddy," Mahira whispered back.

Chapter Three

The cargo lifter hovered steadily three feet above the ground, moving at a blistering pace through the dense foliage of the rainforest. In the cockpit several lights flashed with frenzied beeps, signalling the inbuilt AI was making split second calculations to avoid colliding with the countless trees. Six cargo containers floated on magnetic connecters, all joined to the lifter and forming its tail. In the final container, hidden amongst the various humanitarian aid supply crates, Nishfar crouched with sweat dripping from his brow.

Against the recommendation of Daav'id, and to the mortification of Marie, he had ignored the lock down imposed on the Arcology and smuggled himself onto a convoy heading for the frontline. Marie had feared he would be caught and tried, risking imprisonment at the hands of a legal system living in fear of insurgency. Daav'id on the other hand was more concerned about the ramifications on his own political station, fearing if he was found to have not used all means possible to stop his son-in-law he would be forced to resign. However when Nishfar had told them his intentions his expression had shown such a staunch determination that both of them knew they could not dissuade him.

The cargo lifter made incredibly jarring jinks and turns. No matter how hard he tried to balance himself within the container, Nishfar found himself flung around like a ceramic pinball. He could feel the bruises already forming on his arms and his ribs from the countless collisions he'd made with the surrounding crates. Unable to see outside, Nishfar relied on his hearing to ascertain how close the lifter was to New Arsia. The sounds of conflict were faint at first, but they soon became louder and more ferocious.

Slinging his rucksack on to his back and tightening the straps, Nishfar took a deep breath to calm his nerves. The roar of air brakes penetrated the interior of the cargo container as Nishfar found himself flung backwards against his will. He collided with a wooden crate and fell to his knees. *Once again Neesh, you find yourself hurled like a rag doll. It's quickly becoming a thing,* he thought to himself as he clambered once more to his feet. He could sense the cargo lifter was no longer moving which meant either they had arrived or had otherwise been blocked. If his mental calculations were correct, and they usually were, then he believed it was the former. Sure enough, the hum of the magnetic connectors disengaging followed. Nishfar readied himself as the container dropped three feet, the internal bracers absorbing the brunt of the impact. Almost instantly, the container doors opened.

Covered in varying degrees of blood, sweat and dirt, nearly sixty people stared blankly into the container. Two at the front, wearing government badges, stepped in and proceeded to unpack the humanitarian aid. Nishfar slipped between a gap in the crates, coming face to face with one of the aides.

"What the hell are you doing in here?" she questioned, astonished to find a human being amongst the food, water and clothing supplies.

"Umm," Nishfar responded, his mind working overtime to find an excuse. "Just making sure these supplies made it here OK… They're OK."

A tense few seconds passed as the woman looked at him with a mixture of confusion and disbelief.

Nishfar slowly edged forwards, his expression frozen with a dumb smile. Looking him square in the eye the woman placed a hand on his shoulder as he tried to make his way past.

"Most people smuggle out of conflict," she posited, "you smuggled yourself in. I won't question why, just don't presume me a fool who would believe such an absurd reason for you to be here."

"Sorry," Nishfar responded, nonplussed. "I don't suppose I could ask you a favour?"

"Probably not," the woman responded with a less than impressed glare.

"Where can I find the F.H.A.?" he continued. The woman's expression immediately darkened and she reached for her sidearm, though stopping short of drawing it.

"Why do you ask?" she questioned belligerently. Behind her the crowd gasped with fear, recoiling at the possibility of a weapon being drawn. The other government employee ceased unpacking and stepped forwards, similarly placing his hand upon his sidearm. Nishfar noticeably tensed, raising his hands in front of him to signal them to hold off.

"Because I'm writing a story and I want first-hand experience. People need to know the truth of these individuals!" Nishfar responded. The woman stared at him for a second before noticeably relaxing and removing her hand from her sidearm.

"Bloody journalists. Look, I don't know where you came from or why you risked coming here in such a fashion, but I will tell you this: The F.H.A. should not be trifled with. If you ask around the camp, I'm sure someone will know, but just beware of what you ask," she continued before turning to start unpacking supplies, "because if you ask the wrong person you're liable to be shot."

Ashen grass, damp mud and burnt foliage covered the ground of the refugee camp. The pungent smell of death, dysentery and sulphur filled the air. The sound of explosions and gunfire echoed in the distance as yet another battle ensued in central New Arsia. Each explosion, or the sound of a shell whistling through the air, seemed ever closer and yet still so far away. Nishfar realised there was no peace for this camp, for the refugees evacuated, or forced, from their homes. He realised that had it not been for his influential in-law's, he too would be calling a camp like this his home; although the destruction of New Pavonis had been so horrifyingly thorough that he could not see how enough people could have survived to form a camp.

As Nishfar walked forwards through the main thoroughfare he witnessed men, women and children covered in dirt, many injured and most overcome with despair. One woman, her hair dishevelled and a crudely stitched cut upon her brow, wept uncontrollably over the unconscious body of a man he assumed to be her husband. Nishfar found himself wanting to intervene, to offer some form of help, but as he drew closer he realised that the husband was not unconscious but had passed. Nishfar looked forlornly upon the woman as she briefly gazed in his direction, her eyes frozen with sorrow, before returning her attention to her deceased husband. He shared her pain, more than she would ever know and memories of the fateful night he lost Layla came flooding back. Composing himself and returning to his trudge, Nishfar witnessed a young girl, perceptively not much older than his own Mahira, making mud pies. Her eyes were glazed, with all hope having evaporated from her expression. Taking a moment to pause and look around him, Nishfar realised that not a single person was smiling. Not even the children displayed joy, for whom it should have been second nature. He found himself overcome with melancholy, unable to find the will to ask any of these people if they knew about the F.H.A.

Lumbering over dead vines and past demoralised refugees, a voice called out to him from one of the tents. "Nishfar? Nishfar Montiz, is that you?" The female asked as she emerged from within, her voice conveying a welcome warmth. Nishfar turned around and a smile immediately crossed his lips.

"Dr Cassandra D'cruze," he said with a heartfelt warmth. Cassandra was a childhood friend and one whom Nishfar had not seen for nigh on four years. She had been friends to both him and his brother Keifar, even going on to serve alongside Keifar in the Marines. Where Layla had been the angel on his shoulder, Cass had always been the devil. However, despite her propensity to get Nishfar into trouble, she had always proved herself to be an esteemed friend. A fact he had honoured by naming her the best *'man'* at his wedding.

Walking forwards at pace, tying her hair into a ponytail as she did so, she flung open her arms to embrace him. Likewise, Nishfar welcomed her with a warm hug, the kind reserved only for old friends.

"It's been far too long," Cass said with a smile. "What brings you to New Arsia? Are you volunteering? We need all the help we can get!"

"Unfortunately not," Nishfar responded, releasing her from their embrace. "I'm looking for someone... I'm looking for Keifar."

Cass paused and stared at Nishfar intently, trying to gauge if he was being serious and his expression soon told her as much.

"But Keifar is dead, Nishfar?" she responded, her tone inferring it was a question rather than a point. "Your dad identified his body. Heck my girlfriend treated him. Even she said there was no coming back from what he had been through!"

"How is Darshana?" Nishfar digressed, recalling Cass' old partner in crime.

"We split up around a year past. I asked her to marry me, she said no," Cass continued, clearly pushing aside her emotions, "anyway don't change the subject. Is there something I should know?"

"Can we go somewhere more private?" Nishfar continued, suddenly paranoid at who may be around, who may be listening to his words. Cass grabbed his arm without reply and pulled him towards the tent she had previously been inside.

Various medical supplies dotted the interior and at the centre a single, make shift, steel slab stood covered in blood and in the process of being cleaned by an older woman. Several powered down medical machines surrounded the slab, most of them were decades old and some of them not even used in modern medicine; here they were a commodity. In the corner several yellow bio hazard containers sat covered in equal parts blood and dirt. Most of them were full to near bursting point, sealed by elastasteel couplings.

"Losé, could you give me a few minutes?" Cass politely asked, resting a caring hand upon the older woman's shoulder. Losé nodded and exited the tent, slipping past Nishfar with a smile. Cass quickly dragged out two crude metal stools and motioned for Nishfar to take a seat. Happy to get off his feet, even if it was for the briefest of moments, he sat down and removed his backpack.

"He's not dead," Nishfar responded, bluntly. "It seems he's with the F.H.A."

"How do you know? Has he contacted you?" Cass enquired, clasping her hands together and looking on intently.

"Did you see the news the other night?" Nishfar responded.

"Wait…he is the one that took out the Planetary News First drone?" she questioned, her voice suggesting a little more than a passing concern.

"He was, why do you ask?" Nishfar continued, noticing her unease.

"Because that turned more than a few heads back in the Soleri Arcology. Some very influential people were incredibly…how can I say…displeased by his words," she

35

responded, resting her head in her hands and wiping her face. "I should know…they ordered me to track that guy down."

Chapter Four

It was the middle of the night when screams awoke Nishfar from his sleep. The floor was cold, damp and muddy but it had been a darn sight more comfortable than the steel slab he had been offered. Cass came storming through the tent flap, marched up to the crudely constructed metal medicine cabinet and unlocked it with a key. Nishfar's mind wasn't yet entirely compos mentis and so he looked at her with a mixture of confusion and bewilderment. His mind was brought throttling into reality, however, when the whistle of mortars falling form the sky became dreadfully close. Cass dropped to her knees, pulling Nishfar in as she did so and immediately afterwards the tent was shaken by an explosion. The sound was near deafening, speaking to how incredibly close it was. Another whistle penetrated the air, followed by an equally closer explosion. Outside the screaming intensified.

"Nishfar!" Cass yelled, grabbing his head in her hands, "Nishfar?"

"I'm here, I'm here," he responded, shaking his head and slapping himself twice on the cheeks. "What the hell is going on?"

"We're under attack. Here I need you to hold these for me." Cass responded, dropping a load of medical supplies into his arms and then proceeding to grab what remaining syringes and medicine she could. Nishfar froze. Although his mind raced over everything he would need to do and the various ways he could help, his body did not want to move. Fear gripped his very being. Through his mind thoughts of Mahira raced, then followed the agonising memory of Layla being shot and how powerless he was to save her. "I couldn't save her," he whimpered, his mind regressing. Cass looked at him with heartfelt sorrow. She realised in that moment that she wasn't dealing with a colleague or a squad mate, she was dealing with a civilian. Crouching down in front of him, ignoring the further whistles of mortar fire, she looked him deep in the eyes.

"Nishfar!" she spoke, her tone assertive yet caring, "Nishfar can you hear me?"

He looked at her blankly, his pupils dilated and his heart racing. Cass sighed, she knew what she had to do.

Nishfar found himself flung painfully back to reality as Cass' hand struck him across the right cheek.

"Snap out of it Nishfar, you're better than this!" she commanded.

"I'm sorry Cass, I'm sorry," he responded, shaking himself free of the fear and putting it to the back of his mind.

"I need you now. Losé has been killed and I don't have another nurse," she continued, "I know you're not one but you've read enough books to have a better idea than anyone else here."

Her words spoke a great deal of truth. One of Nishfar's strengths, his passion, was to read. His study back in New Pavonis had nearly one thousand books, most of which were non-fiction and they weren't all on colonial history. Several of them had been on human biology, first aid and medicine, for at one time, shortly after university, medicine drew his attention. Before Nishfar could respond, another explosion rocked the tent causing two of the legs to collapse and forcing the tarpaulin in on its self.

"We have to move, keep your head down low, follow me and do not deviate," Cass commanded, her words carrying an authority he had never witnessed from her, something she had clearly learned in the Marines. Nishfar nodded and the pair slowly crouched towards the tent flap.

Outside, the camp had descended into pure chaos as all around refugees scrambled for non-existent cover. Many tents were ablaze; men, women and children scrambling from within, struggling with injuries, or clawing away in a vain attempt to secure personal belongings. Several mercenaries stood, Las-Carbines in hand, motioning to refugees to take cover or leading them away from fires. Less than one klick due north the sounds of lasgun fire intensified, mixed with unconventional firearms and the sound Nishfar had come to despise; railguns. Cass signalled for them to move south, a move that brought a degree of relief to Nishfar, as much comfort as a man could get in a live conflict zone.

"Why are they attacking us?" Nishfar questioned as the pair moved through the tents, keeping low to stay out of sight,

"Who knows?" Cass yelled. "But this is the first time they have sent ground troops against us in at least four weeks." The pair made their way toward a break in the tree line at the rear of the camp. Four mercenaries had gathered with a group of women and children.

As Nishfar advanced on the group he realised the situation was dire. Several of the children were heavily wounded with one young boy, probably no older than Mahira, having lost his hand. Nishfar felt his stomach unbalance at the sight of so much blood and it took all his willpower not to vomit. Cass immediately dived to her knees beside the young boy, dropping the medicine into a pile. He was unconscious in the arms of his mother, her dirt ridden dress covered in his blood. Nishfar held back his shock and equally dived to his knees. "Hold the arm!" Cass shouted. To which Nishfar quickly took hold of the boy and his injured arm. "Raise it. It'll help ease the bleeding," Cass continued, preparing a syringe with a dose of anaesthetic for the boy. Nishfar lifted the boys arm as Cass checked his pulse and then administered the injection. Without missing a beat she then reached into the pile of medical supplies Nishfar had been carrying and retrieved two clasps and a Medifoam canister. With practised precision, she used pliers to apply a clasp to the ulnar and radial arteries, staunching the flow of blood. Once secured, she then applied the Medifoam which sealed the stump of the wrist and stopped the rest of the bleeding.

"That'll protect him until we can get him into surgery," Cass said, placing a caring hand upon the mother's shoulder. "Stars be with us, he'll be OK." Another explosion rocked tents near the tree line and further screams echoed out throughout the night. Two of the mercenaries, whom had been protecting the small group, raised their carbines and aimed towards the area in which the most recent explosion had occurred.

There was a momentary pause, Nishfar froze again. He recognised the electrical charge that reverberated through the air and he found the world around him blur. Without due care for himself he leapt to his feet, dived and took both mercenaries to the ground with him. Seconds later the trees behind where they had stood erupted into flame as railgun fire tore through them.

"What the fuck!" one of the mercenaries exclaimed, looking at Nishfar with a glare that could melt ice. He was soon silenced by his squad mate who clipped him around the back of the head.

"Show some respect, that guy just saved your ass!" he shouted. The pair then rolled onto their chests and aimed their carbines back at the assailants. Nishfar signalled for Cass to get the children deeper into the rainforest, regardless of the risks. Cass could see the fear in his eyes and the intent. She knew he had borne witness to this scenario before. Without question she gathered the injured women and children, beginning to martial them deeper into the tree line.

A moment of silence covered the camp. The mortar fire ceased and the distant sounds of laser fire had all but evaporated. All that could be heard was the sound of roaring flame, as the fires tore through sections of the camp, and Nishfar's staggered breathing. One of the mercenaries slapped him on the shoulder and signalled for him to be quieter, by placing his finger to his lips. At the same time his squad mate reached down, removed his sidearm from its holster and passed it to Nishfar. Nishfar hated guns with a passion, knowing full well the evils they had brought upon Earth and, later, her colonies. When his brother and Cass had joined the Marines he protested heavily against them training to use such weapons, protests that fell on deaf ears. Now he found himself in a conflict zone with one offered to him, facing a potential enemy who cared little whether he was armed or not. Much to his surprise Nishfar found himself taking hold of the weapon. With a book learned competence he checked the chamber for a round, checked the clip and removed the safety. For a moment, the mercenary looked at him, shocked. The three of them were brought hurtling back to the present when railgun fire tore into the tree line once again. "Cover fire!" one of the mercenaries yelled, opening up with burst fire from his Las-Carbine. His squad mate immediately did the same. Sounds of red hot light colliding with metal echoed throughout the vicinity.

Nishfar raised his head to see what was occurring, and his heart sank. Advancing on them were two warriors in black metallic armour, the same type worn by those who killed Layla. Nishfar wasn't sure what came over him, but he immediately opened fire. His bullets struck home, but they were useless against the armour warn by the assailants. One of the mercenaries grabbed him by the scruff of the neck and pulled him back. "Calm down! That gun won't do shit against them!" he yelled. "Hold this!"

The mercenary quickly handed Nishfar his Las-Carbine before unclasping his gun belt and removing a knife from within his boot. Nishfar stared at him with a mixture of confusion and disbelief. "And you think a Knife will work?" he questioned, unsure of what he was witnessing. "No. But I spied a Fusion Cell, positioned just above the neck joint. If I jam my knife in there, it'll cause a reaction that'll result in total breakdown," the mercenary continued, "then they'll be lambs to the slaughter!" his squad mate interjected.

"On my mark, start moving right and firing. Keep low. Once you have their attention, I'll flank left and do my thing!" the mercenary continued, gripping the knife in his teeth. He raised his hand, displaying all four digits and his thumb before proceeding to retract them one by one. When the last one lowered, he motioned for his squad mate to move out.

Nishfar watched on with equal parts anxiety and awe. The mercenaries worked with a practiced precision, but on this occasion it wasn't entirely enough. As his colleague was flanking to the left, the distractor was caught twice in the chest. He stumbled to his knees and yet kept firing, willing himself to his feet to go that little bit further. Seeing his friend get shot spurred the knife wielder on and he leapt a good six feet, landing on the back of one of the armoured warriors. Wrestling with the mercenary in a vain attempt to get him off his back, the warrior struggled to no avail. With rage in his eyes the mercenary stabbed the knife into the fusion cell, sparks and flame bursting forth. He'd acted with such fury that he hadn't given himself enough time to recover. The second of the armoured warriors turned around, took hold of him with his clamp and gripped tightly. Nishfar watched on in abstract fear as the man was crushed to death, blood pouring from his mouth. Realising his ally was compromised, the second armoured warrior flung the lifeless corpse of the mercenary to the ground and then proceeded to stand in front of him to provide cover. But it wouldn't be enough. From within the tree line, a huge burst of flame shot forth, launching from within it a warhead the size of a small crate. It collided with the armoured warriors, exploding with a bright flash and a huge ball of fire. Nishfar instinctively ducked, the burning shrapnel flying overhead and impaling the foliage. The two combatants were down and for the first time, Nishfar wished they were those that had killed his wife.

Chapter Five

Dawn broke over the camp. Sat upon a metal stool outside Cass' tent, Nishfar was exhausted. The scholar remained awake through force of will and a little extra help from the copious amounts of coffee he had drunk. His hands were dry with the blood of those he had helped throughout the night. It had been tough and he had witnessed more horrors than a man should have to in his lifetime; but it was all for a good cause. Cass had been without a single nurse and so Nishfar had stepped up to the plate where no one else could. If it wasn't for his willingness to support he knew many more would have perished at the hand of war.

Hands clasped tightly around his thermos, the coffee within causing steam to rise into the cool morning air, he stared out across the ruin that had befallen the refugee camp. Yesterday it had been a dark place filled with sorrow and despondence, this morning it was furthermore bleak. All around him men, women and children struggled to gather what little belongings had survived the raging infernos. Elsewhere people grieved over the burned, beaten or shot ridden bodies of their loved ones. Behind him, to the side of Cass' tent, near forty bodies lay covered by tarpaulin and identified only by a tag; those that Cass couldn't save. Nishfar looked dejected as he took a further sip of his coffee, ignorant to its heat as it burned his throat. Seeing the pain as a form of penance for those he could not help save.

The tent flaps flung open as Cass emerged, surgical mask around her neck and sweat dripping from her forehead; her Theatre Blues covered in dirt and blood. She wiped her brow with her arm before removing her surgical gloves, flinging them onto a pile that had amassed in the mud outside. Nishfar looked at her with inquisitive eyes. Cass shook her head in response. The pair then stared once more across the camp, their eyes filled with mourning. Standing from his stool Nishfar took a step towards Cass, placed a hand on her shoulder and passed her the coffee. She smiled at him, displaying her continuing endurance against the hardships of this stars forsaken war.

"You did all you could," Nishfar spoke with a reassuring smile.

"My all wasn't enough," Cass responded, clasping her hands tightly around the thermos. "My all couldn't save her, I couldn't save those thirty eight other women and children."

"No one could!' Nishfar responded with an unexpected forcefulness. "This war is responsible for their deaths, not you."

Cass looked dejected yet she nodded in response. Nishfar could see she understood what he was saying, but the truth was still hard to take in the face of such adversity.

"I owe you an explanation," she continued, having taken more than a mouthful of coffee.

"You don't have to explain to me now," Nishfar responded, maintaining a reassuring hand upon her shoulder.

"Yes I do. I let you sleep on the knowledge I was hunting the man you believe to be your brother, my friend. Through a night that could have resulted in your death or mine!" she continued, her expression filled with a fiery passion Nishfar knew not to contend.

"Very well. Why are you hunting him?" he questioned, once more sitting down on his stool. Cass pulled another one out from within the tent and sat beside him, passing the coffee back. Nishfar signalled for her to keep it.

"Originally I was not here to volunteer. I was here on assignment," she acknowledged. "About a year ago I was honourably discharged from the Marines. Following that I was reassigned to the Office of Planetary Affairs…"

"Spooks?" Nishfar interjected.

"As I was saying, the Office of Planetary Affairs," Cass continued with a smirk, clearly agreeing without saying as much. "I was assigned to Dignitary Support. Which is O.P.A. code for Secret Service. On the surface we travel with, support and protect government officials or those of corporate interest. But the truth is we are, as you so eloquently put it; Spooks."

Nishfar nodded, fascinated by what Cass was divulging. Clearly something had implored her to reveal this to him, information he feared could get her into trouble should it be discovered.

"My handler sent word to me, following the invasion of New Pavonis, that I was to hunt a man code named The Hawk," Cass continued, looking at Nishfar intently. "That man, the man they call 'The Hawk', is the leader of the F.H.A."

Nishfar paused, his expression a mixture of consternation and bewilderment. "You think Keifar is this 'Hawk'?" he posited.

"If you are certain that he is the man you saw on the news broadcast the other night, then I am certain he is 'The Hawk'!" Cass responded, her eyes speaking volumes. "Because mere moments after that broadcast I was contacted by my handler, a man I had not heard from in months, and he issued a Reticence Order!"

Fully aware of the definition of Reticence, Nishfar immediately surmised the nature of the order and his face filled with a degree of shock. "The O.P.A. want to kill Keifar!" he responded, his tone tinged with righteous indignation. "And you're the weapon?"

Cass' head dropped and she gave a feint nod. "You truly weren't here to volunteer were you?" Nishfar continued, becoming fully aware of the truth that now confronted him. "You were here to gather intelligence on 'The Hawk', to discover his whereabouts and with that information, kill him," Nishfar continued, his words imbued with a sense of disappointment. Resigned, Cass' eyes remained fixed on the ground in front of her.

Nishfar paused. He looked out across the devastation of the camp once more, unsure how to respond. He was disturbed to discover how far his friend had fallen. The once kind hearted, ever protective Cassandra D'cruze had become a trained killer. Ordered to kill for people protected by the gilded cage of government. Yet all last night he had witnessed the Cass he remembered, a woman who would sacrifice her very life for others, the doctor he knew and cared deeply for. "So you were going to find him, and then kill him?" Nishfar questioned, his tone expecting an honest response.

"I cannot lie and say I wasn't," Cass responded, her tone dejected, "but I can promise you this. I would never have pulled the trigger on Keifar!"

"Would you have had time to learn it was him?" Nishfar questioned, his tone forlorn,

"Honestly? We'll never know. But now I am aware it is Keifar, I won't kill him. He deserves a chance to answer for his supposed crimes, to face a fair trial in our courts." Nishfar started laughing, his reaction perplexing to Cass.

"You know full well that if the government put a Reticence Order on him they don't want him to speak, they want him dead. He'd never receive a fair trial," Nishfar continued, still unable to make eye contact with his old friend.

"I fear you may be right!" Cass responded with a defeated melancholy. "You may be right."

For nearly ten minutes the pair of them shared an uncomfortable silence, their eyes scanning the camp yet never facing each other. Nishfar's expression was dejected, his heart unsure how to feel. Cass, on the other hand, was torn between the government she swore to serve, and the friends she had grown up with. "You know you have a choice to make?" Nishfar spoke, breaking the silence.

"I know," Cass responded, her tone crestfallen.

"I can't take you with me to find my brother if you're going to bring him home, or worse," Nishfar continued, standing from his stool. "He's the only hope I have of getting Mahira to safety. I won't let you jeopardise that Cass, I can't let you jeopardise that!"

"I would expect nothing less," Cass smiled, finally matching eye line with her old friend. "Latest intel puts him under the old Marine barracks, North East of the settlement. You can use a four wheeler to get there, the Merc's don't password protect ignition so they're easy to *'borrow'*." Nishfar walked past Cass, placing a hand on her shoulder and squeezing fondly. His grip speaking a thousand words when his mouth said none.

Back inside the tent, Nishfar was confronted by a distressing scene. The makeshift surgical theatre was covered in blood, surgical tools and medical supplies strewn across any surface that could hold them. On the steel slab the deceased body of a nine year old girl laid, her chest heavily wounded by laser fire and stitched by Cass in the vain attempt to save her life. Stood beside her, overlooking the lifeless body, tears streaming down their cheeks, her parents looked on in anguish. Nishfar exchanged an apologetic look with the father who nodded with thanks. The disgruntled scholar then proceeded to remove his scrubs and gather his things. "Are you leaving?" A sorrowful female voice called out. Nishfar turned around to find both Mother and Father looking at him expectantly.

"I have somewhere I need to be," he responded, removing a clean shirt from his backpack.

"But what will Cass do without you? There are many more walking wounded. Without a nurse she will struggle!" the mother continued.

"She will be OK, she is more talented than you give her credit for. Plus, more volunteers will come," Nishfar responded, trying to keep his tone positive as he removed his t-shirt and put on the clean one removed from his bag.

"You don't know that for sure," the father said. "You can't." Nishfar's eyes filled with sorrow, although he hid as much by facing the wall. The father's words spoke true, he didn't know that for sure. But he couldn't stay, he had to find his brother. If not for him, then for Mahira. With his new shirt on, he raised his backpack over his shoulder and turned to face the parents.

"You're right, I can't know that for sure," he continued, walking towards the exit to the tent. "But I have faith, and you must too. In these darkest of days, faith is all we have."

Outside the tent Cass had not moved, still holding a thermos now empty of coffee. Nishfar placed a hand on her shoulder, once more grasping her fondly. "These people need you Cass, they need someone who can look out for them like you can," Nishfar spoke, his words filled with veneration. "Regardless of what has been asked of you I know, in my heart, you will do what is right!" he continued, letting go and walking off towards the camp's carpool. Cass didn't respond, her eyes unreservedly following him as he walked away. Her crestfallen expression speaking of a conflict in her very heart; between what she must do, what she wanted to do, and what she was asked to do. Nishfar had faith his old friend would do the right thing, but she needed to make that decision for herself. If anyone else did, her heart would always be conflicted.

The carpool was devoid of activity. Very few mercenaries stood guard, having been drawn into the rebuilding of the camp following the attack. Four remained. Two in the temporary watch tower that had been erected to look over the entirety of the camp, and its surroundings, and two milling around near the four wheelers. Of the two near the four wheelers only one held a Las-Carbine, the other smoking a snake skin cigar, rare on Hakon IV. Nishfar crouched down behind one of the four wheelers and peaked over the driver side door. He was looking for one with code ignition, not key card, and to his distaste the first was card. Nishfar continued on, checking the second, third and forth in the line, each of them card ignition. *Come on Cass! You said they never password protect ignition, yet none of these are code ignition*, he thought to himself, slumping to the ground, defeated. The four remaining four wheelers were right next to the two mercenaries, and within line of sight of the tower. Near impossible for him to access, start and escape without being confronted; but he had to try.

Dropping prone, he crawled through the mud to the other line of vehicles, his relatively clean shirt quickly sullied. Rising to a crouch by the passenger door, he held his breath as he peered over the top. To his joy a key pad to the left of the drivers console identified it as code ignition. The two mercenaries, who were exchanging views of last night's conflict, stood mere feet away and certainly within hearing range. Quietly Nishfar placed his backpack in the back seat and slowly opened the door to the driver's seat. Edging in slowly, he closed the door behind him with a tense noiselessness. Cowered as lowly as he could be in an open topped four wheeler, he reached down toward the keypad and pressed ignition. The engine roared into action, both merc's turned instinctively, one of them raising his Las-Carbine. Nishfar was ready to shift the vehicle into gear and move out when he felt the cold metal of a Las-Carbine barrel pressed firmly against the back of his head. Instinctively he raised his hands. "And where do you think you're going son?" a grizzled voice questioned. Nishfar's heart sank.

"To get much needed medical supplies!" a familiar voice responded, her voice relieving Nishfar's fears. Cass opened the passenger door, slinging her own backpack into the back seat.

"He's with me Seb, lower you gun!" she continued. Nishfar looked at her, a faint smile crossing his lips.

"Thank you," he mouthed, his expression filled with relief. Smiling back at him she looked to the gun wielding mercenary as he retracted his gun from the back of Nishfar's head.

"We'll be back in a couple of days, Dr Hannover just arrived and will look after the sick. However he might need a little assistance, his hover chair doesn't fare well in these conditions."

"Sure thing Doc!" the mercenary responded, his voice filled with a respectful grit. Cass turned to Nishfar and smiled. "Let's get this party on the road then, Neesh!"

***

The drive through New Arsia was long. Every street they passed through, every corner they turned, and every tunnel traversed was lifeless. It was a ghost settlement covered in the scars of war, white smoke rising from destroyed Hab-blocks and burned out vehicles, both military and civilian. The road ways were covered in the rubble and ruin of conflict, putting the four wheelers suspension through its paces. Nishfar's hands gripped the wheel firmly, his eyes darting between the road ahead and the digital read out on the Holo-Screen of the driver's console.

"You've been silent since we left. Are you not going to ask me why I am here?" Cass spoke breaking the monotonous silence that had befallen the pair. Nishfar didn't respond, retaining his focus on the road ahead. "In all my years I have never known Nishfar Montiz to remain so quiet," she jested, a smirk crossing her lips. Nishfar's expression brightened.

"Ah ha!" Cass exclaimed. "There is life in him yet!"

"I didn't need to ask you why you are here," he muttered, "because there are only two possible reasons. You want to help, or you want to kill my brother," Cass' eyes narrowed, suspicious of where Nishfar was going with this line of thinking.

"And I know, deep down in your heart, you don't want to kill Keifar. Which means you're here to help," he smiled, exchanging a brief glance with her. Cass diverted her gaze in order to hide her cheeks and the subsequent blush, but Nishfar could tell she was embarrassed. "As for remaining silent," he continued. "Layla always used to say that when I drive, if I talk, I don't pay attention to the road."

"How is Layla?" Cass questioned. "You haven't spoken about her once since you arrived." Nishfar's expression darkened, a lesser seen sorrow filling his eyes. Cass instinctively knew something bad had happened, and she placed a reassuring hand on his arm.

"It's OK," she said, gripping him fondly as he had done so to her earlier. "What happened?"

Nishfar slammed on the breaks, skidding to a halt by the side of the road, his eyes welling up. Cass was overcome with surprise, her empathy starting to absorb some of his pain, her eyes reacting with the same sorrow as his. "You don't have to tell me if you don't want to," she continued. "Not if it's too painful for you."

"They killed her!" he near shouted. "The armoured warriors, the ones that also attacked the camp, they killed her!" he continued, his tone broken and tinged with sorrow. "I couldn't save her. I couldn't save them!" For the first time since that fateful night, when Layla died in his arms, Nishfar broke down. The sheer force of his emotions erupting in a stream of emotional pain and tears. Such was his anguish that Cass, too, found herself in tears, reaching over and grabbing him in a hug.

The intensity of Nishfar's grief had finally broken down the walls he had constructed to contain it. The harder he cried, the tighter Cass held him, letting him truly grieve for the first time since Layla's death.

"In the attack on the Arcology?" Cass questioned, rocking him in her arms. "During the breach?"

"She was one of nearly six thousand casualties. One of the four thousand and eighty six dead," he responded, "I left her with Mahira, under the stairs, with her parents. Whilst I went outside in the vain belief I could help people; the vain belief I could help them unlike the night the sky turned red."

Cass held him tighter, tears now streaming from her own eyes as she shared in his pain.

"She opened the door. She came to check on me. To see if I was safe," he continued, his voice breaking with every word. "It was there, in the door way, as she smiled at me. It was there that they gunned her down. I cradled her in my arms. I watched her die. My clothes drenched in her blood. How do I forget that? How do I forget that I couldn't save her?"

"The truth is, you don't," Cass responded, her tone displaying a candour many would not use in such an emotional situation. But Cass knew Nishfar, and she knew he would expect nothing less from her. "But what you can do Neesh?" she continued. "You can use that pain, use it to fight for Mahira. She is all that matters now!"

"Her and Keifar," Nishfar whimpered.

"You and me both know Keifar can look after himself. We didn't call him Ass-Kicker for nothing!" Cass responded, the pair of them chuckling at the recollection of his childhood nickname; a name that quickly became his call sign in the Marines. The brief moment of mirth provided a much needed break in the pain.

Ten minutes passed as the pair sat in the four wheeler, their expressions returning from the dark sorrow they had given release to. Abruptly one of the doorways, an old design, non-automatic, outward opening one, sprang open. "Head down!" Cass whispered, her tone taking on a commanding edge once more. Immediately Nishfar ducked in his seat, wiping the remaining tears from his eyes. With her own head ducked down Cass reached into the back seat, to her backpack, and retrieved her personal side arm. Nishfar looked at it and perceptively shook his head, raising his hand to lower hers. She raised a finger to her mouth to signal for him to be quiet. "Trust me," she whispered, her tone barely audible. Nishfar shook his head yet retracted his arm. Seconds later four heavily armed men, garbed all in black and wielding long range Las-Rifles, appeared from the door. With trained military precision they took up firing positions outside the door. Once secure they signalled back in the doorway and emerging from within came an older man dressed in a long black trench coat, military style peaked cap, with a scar running through his right eye. That same eye was clearly cybernetic and it assessed his surroundings with inhuman speed. "Shit!" Cass whispered, to which Nishfar looked at her blankly,

"Insurgents. A Commander no less. This is problematic," she continued, noticeably removing the safety on her sidearm. Nishfar noticeably tensed,

51

"Not F.H.A?" he questioned.

"Unfortunately not," she responded. "Something I never thought I'd say."

The insurgent commander strolled amongst his contingent with an assured sense of self-importance. He reached inside his coat to retrieve a cigar, giving a momentary glimpse of his sidearm, a revolver with an oversized barrel.

"Somebody is overcompensating. With that monstrosity," Nishfar whispered, to which Cass could barely hold back a chuckle. Lighting the cigar in his mouth with a suitably grandiose zippo lighter, the commander gave off an iniquitous smile. He began speaking, but was at such a range that neither Nishfar nor Cass could hear what he was saying. Cass grunted with annoyance, prompting Nishfar to look at her inquisitively.

"I may be defying a direct order to kill your brother. But I still serve this government," she posited, responding to his expression. "They might have much needed intel. Intel that could save lives!" She proceeded to unlock the side door at which point Nishfar grabbed her arm and looked her dead in the eyes.

"This isn't our job," he whispered, his eyes pleading with her not to get out.

"Correction. This isn't your job. It's mine!" she responded with a passionate indignation Nishfar knew he could not contend. "Stay here."

Like a ghost, Cass was gone in mere seconds. Despite the sweltering suns shining down upon the scorched ruins of New Arsia she was nowhere to be seen, a testament to her training. Nishfar watched the group of insurgents with an eagle eye, careful to remain unnoticed. His heart was racing although he did his best to calm himself. The tension he felt could be cut with nothing less than a chainsaw. Unanticipatedly the commander looked directly at the four wheeler, his expression displaying a perturbed curiosity. Nishfar pushed himself as low as he could without breaking his ribs, fear creeping in. Without a single word spoken the commander gestured for two of his four man contingent to advance upon the four wheeler with him. As he moved forward he withdrew the oversized revolver from its holster at his waist, and gritted the cigar in his teeth, using both hands to steady his aim.

"Is there anyone in there?" he questioned, his voice gruff and aged by war. "Come out with your hands up!" Nishfar was frozen by fear again. Cass was nowhere to be seen and he feared, after all he had witnessed, if he removed himself from the safety of the four wheeler he would be gunned down where he stood. As a result he stayed low and did not respond, instead moving his hand toward the ignition keypad, ready to start her up at a moment's notice.

However before the insurgent commander and his two man contingent could reach the four wheeler one of the men that had remained behind cried out in pain. All three individuals turned around. Stood with her knife imbedded deep in between the neck and shoulder of the man, his compatriot deceased on the floor, Cass looked on with furious intent. The insurgent commander raised his gun, as did his compatriots and glared in her direction. Intelligently Cass had placed their colleague between her and them, offering her what she believed to be a position from which she could negotiate. However the insurgent commander soon proved himself the nefarious being he appeared to be. With little care, and even less remorse, he shot her human shield, his man, in the head. Shock took hold of Cass as the body dropped toward the ground, blood and grey matter covering her darkening expression of shock. The commander began to laugh sadistically, his compatriots joining in half-heartedly. "The key to hostage taking, my dear, is that the hostage must have some degree of emotional attachment to those you seek to bargain with," the commander spoke with an assured sense of victory. "My men, although useful, are not without replacements and are trained as such." Cass froze, the knife gripped firmly in her hand, fully expecting the worst, but to her relief, the roar of the four wheelers engine broke the tense silence.

Nishfar did not look, eyes fixed firmly upon the holovid display of the drivers console. He put his foot down, not once lowering the pressure. The firm thud of a collision, followed by the red warning alert on the holovid display informed Nishfar he had connected with the insurgents, but still he could not look. He popped his head up just in time to swerve to the side of Cass who was still frozen. Prepared to die.

"GET IN!" Nishfar yelled. "WE HAVE TO GO!"

"You don't have to tell me twice!" Cass responded, leaping over the door rather than taking the time to open it. Nishfar slammed his foot down once more, the sound of gunfire echoing out behind them. The dink of bullets and laser fire striking metal signalled the survivors shots were on target. They were danger close. Paying no attention to the holovid display, which was still giving directions to the old Marine barracks, Nishfar pulled a hard right off the main boulevard and into a side lane. As he did so he felt the sharp, near agonising pain of a bullet piercing his shoulder. He cried out as the car swerved around the corner, his right arm losing grip as the searing pain overwhelmed him. Cass reflexively reached across and grabbed the steering wheel.

"Direction set: Marine Barracks. Avoid set: Central Boulevard," she yelled, the holovid display identifying her instructions and resetting the route with swift confirmation. "Driver Assist Set: Auto-Drive, Max Speed Set: Thirty miles per hour." Without pause the four wheeler took control of the steering, and Nishfar was quick to grasp his shoulder.

Unaffected by the calculated yet seemingly erratic auto-drive of the four wheeler, Cass set about removing her medical supplies from her back pack. "I had prepared for someone to get shot," Cass jested. "Honestly didn't think it would be you Neesh."

"This is not the time of humour," Nishfar grunted, trying to hold back a smirk. "I'm bleeding out here!"

"Don't be such a cry baby," Cass continued, steadying herself against the undulation. "On that note I'm about to Medifoam you. I'm not going to lie, this is going to sting like a bitch." Unceremoniously she ripped open Nishfar's shirt, flinging the remnant out of the four wheeler and to the dirt. Before Nishfar could lament she pushed the Medifoam dispenser into the wound and released the toggle. Agony overwhelmed him, the kind he had never before felt, not even when he was clipped by the railguns the night he lost Layla. Unable to hold back the vocal outburst that followed, he found himself cursing to the stars. Powerless to maintain a professional bedside manner, Cass began to chuckle.

Her moment of cheerfulness took Nishfar by surprise and he soon quietened.

"You find me being shot that hilarious?" The disgruntled scholar questioned, a degree of enmity in his tone. Despite his hostile inflection, Cass continued chuckling. It didn't take long before her blithe manner brushed off on him. Nishfar too began to laugh, the pair of them letting the adrenaline of the last fifteen minutes bleed out through their guffaw. As their laughter settled, Nishfar looked Cass straight in the eye and she knew what he was about to ask. "Did you find out what you were looking for?" he questioned, as she began to bandage his wounded shoulder.

"Yes," she responded bluntly. "I found out I need to talk to Keifar."

Chapter Six

The tension in the four wheeler was palpable. Nishfar was nursing a wounded shoulder and an equally wounded heart, unsure of what the future held. Cass was fostering a deep secret she insisted she couldn't share until she spoke to Keifar, her eyes and her expression both frozen with the faintest air of dread. Both of them had not shared a word in nearly twenty minutes, neither of them even exchanging a glance; it was as if a wedge had been driven between them. For Nishfar it was because he suddenly felt like Cass didn't trust him, after everything they had experienced. Cass on the other hand was doing it with Nishfar's best interests at heart. Because the information she now held, if it were discovered to be the truth, would be detrimental to his already fragile frame of mind.

The four wheeler had plotted a near direct course despite Cass programming it to avoid the most obvious route to the other side of the settlement. Thirty minutes after being shot, Nishfar watched as the four wheeler skidded into the remnant of the New Arsia Marine base. Prefab military buildings, Hab-Blocks and garages lay in ruin. Long since abandoned as conflict engulfed the settlement and the call to reinforce New Peraea, and the Soleri Arcology, was made. Dotted around the remnant of the base, skeletal corpses lay strewn across the ground. What little flesh remained charred beyond recognition. Nishfar turned off the ignition and proceeded to clamber out, clearly burdened by the gunshot wound in his shoulder. Undoing Nishfar's work, Cass triggered the ignition once more as she proceeded to get out. "Direction Set: Indefinite, Due North. Driver Assist Set: Auto-Drive. Max Speed Set: seventy miles per hour," she commanded, slamming the door as she did so. Nishfar barely had his backpack out of the rear seat before the four wheeler burst into life, disappearing off in a northerly direction. Nishfar was about to question her reasoning for getting rid of their one method of escape then his educated mind broke free of the pain and identified the reasoning; a classic smoke and mirrors manoeuvre.

"The tunnel access is in the Admin Block," Cass commanded, her tone cold and calculating. Speaking to the weight of the secret she now bore. "We should make haste. If my calculations are correct, and they usually are, the insurgents will be boarding flyers as we speak and tracing the trajectory of the Four Wheeler," she continued, removing the four component pieces of her Las-Carbine from her backpack and quickly assembling them without as much as a glance.

"How can you be sure?" Nishfar questioned, grunting as he struggled to hook his backpack over his wounded shoulder.

"Because that's what I would do!" she responded, with an expression that told Nishfar not to question her again. "Let's move."

Nishfar found himself once more on the precipice of questioning, his inquisitive nature breaking free of his pain filled demeanour. But he knew from Cass' present disposition that such questioning would merely result in an apathetic, default response. Instead he fell into step behind her like an ever loyal companion. With practiced military precision that spoke of years in the Marines, Cass raised her Las-Carbine, removed the safety and advanced toward the Admin Block.

She rounded each corner first with disciplined professionalism, checking her firing angles and confirming it was clear, before signalling for Nishfar to move up. He held the sidearm he'd been given earlier with his one good arm, though the pain caused tremors that would make his aim near useless.

Abruptly Cass signalled for Nishfar to stop and the wounded scholar did so without a second's thought. Ahead of them, white smoke signalling a recent and now extinguished fire, stood the partial remains of the admin block; several walls and the main door still intact. Outside the fresh corpses of insurgent soldiers, not dissimilar to those faced earlier, lay lifeless their carcasses pierced by high powered Las fire. Cass moved forwards carefully, never remaining focused on one direction for more than a few seconds, her eyes assessing each and every possible scenario with a skilled situational awareness. As the pair moved forward, Nishfar knelt down beside one of the bodies and placed his hand to its head.

"Still warm, I estimate less than an hour dead. Give or take thirty minutes," he said, his tone macabre.

"We need to move!" Cass whispered. "Something's not right here."

"You don't have to tell me twice," Nishfar responded, quickly standing to his feet and moving in close.

Cass opened the door to the admin block cautiously and quietly, quickly ducking to a knee inside and checking her corners. "Clear!" she commanded with a whisper, signalling for Nishfar to enter in behind her. "Close the door!"

Inside the pair of them were confronted by further signs of recent conflict. The charred, battered, and shot remains of insurgent soldiers littering the hallway. Nishfar studied the scene with an educated eye, immediately noting what had befallen these unfortunate warriors. "Bottleneck," he whispered.

"Yes," Cass responded, "and a prepared one at that, see the scorch marks here and here, those were I.E.D's."

"Motion laser triggered, I'd guess," he said with a sudden assured sense of his own intelligence. Cass looked at him, a smirk finally infiltrating her placid expression for the briefest of seconds.

"What gives you that opinion?" she questioned, eager to know how Nishfar, a man notoriously anti-war, knew of such weapons. Nishfar looked at her with a glint in his eye and strolled forwards, toward one of the bodies.

"The direction of the wounds sustained on his leg here, and his thigh here, suggest an upward blast," he described, gesticulating with the gun held by his one good arm. "The immediacy of angle suggests that no attempt to dodge was made. Ergo, motion laser. One step. BANG!"

Cass and Nishfar froze. He had let his eagerness get the best of him as his closing words echoed throughout the remnant of the building. Both of them waited with trepidation, the sweat noticeably dripping from their brows. Mere moments seemed like an eternity as Nishfar's eyes darted all about him and Cass frantically checked her corners. As seconds turned into minutes, the pair refused to move. Eventually Cass openly sighed and her expression of relief brought a wave of the same to Nishfar; but her countenance soon reverted to one of dissatisfaction.

"Don't… Do that… Again!" She whispered with a suitably sore tone.

"Lesson learned," Nishfar responded with a feeble shrug, markedly hindered by his wound. With a vexed glare, Cass signalled for Nishfar to get behind her again. Not willing to anger his friend any more, he obliged, ducking in behind her like a chastised puppy.

It didn't take long for the pair of them to find the basement access. It was a thick, single access, steel door with attached key pad. The entirety of its front and surrounding walls were covered in signs of battle, with streaks of blood and scorch marks plastered across it. A trail of blood signalled a body had been dragged up to and no doubt beyond it. Both Nishfar and Cass surmised that an individual that had lost that much blood would rarely survive battlefield conditions without immediate Medi-Tank submersion, something reserved only for the affluent or secure military facilities.

"Nishfar, you're up," Cass signalled, turning to take up a firing position facing back down the corridor.

"Sorry, what?" Nishfar questioned, taken aback by her order.

"Get us through that door. You're the brains. Do the brainiac thing!" she continued, hiding from him the moderately entertained smirk that had crossed her lips. Nishfar looked at the console with a mixture of confusion, disbelief, and calculated curiosity. It was a military grade, seven chevron, combination code with ten possible chevrons, each only selectable once in any given entry. Nishfar quickly estimated that it had six hundred and four thousand, eight hundred possible permutations. Without knowing the exact combination, were he to try each possible combination accounting for an average one minute per input, it would take him approximately four hundred and twenty days.

"Cass?" he questioned, to which she looked at him expectantly. "Do we have four hundred and twenty days?"

She frowned disapprovingly, unappreciative of his sarcasm at the juncture. "I figured as much. Ergo, we may wish to find another way through this door," he concluded, shrugging his shoulders.

"Or we could just try my access codes!" she smirked, walking over with her own assured sense of superiority. "Good maths though!" Nishfar felt aggrieved but he could not help but applaud her tenacity. A respectful smirk crossed his lips.

Sure enough Cass' access codes still worked, further confirming the expediency with which the Marines had vacated the facility. The door slid open with a blood curdling grind that sent shivers down even the battle worn Marine's spine. Cass moved inside once more, with practiced skill, as her training took over again. The stair well beyond was dark, all fusion lighting removed or destroyed. Nishfar was immediately reminded of the brief news footage that led to the realisation his brother was still alive. The Planetary News First drone had ventured down a stairwell not dissimilar to this, and no doubt the corridors of the base would be similar to the ones it had traversed as well. Cass paused, switching the under barrel torch of her Las-Carbine to full beam. Both of them were shocked by what the light illuminated. Nishfar so much so that what little contents remained in his stomach were forcibly ejected onto the wall beside him.

Six bodies, or what had clearly once been bodies, lay strewn about the stair case. Each of them was eviscerated, torn asunder or severely mutilated beyond recognition. The pungent smell of dried blood, human entrails and bodily fluids filled the air. Each of the walls were dripping with human remains, even the ceiling hadn't escaped the massacre. Cass was frozen. She had experienced war, had seen squad-mates and civilians alike wounded on the battlefield, but never before had she witnessed such incomprehensible violence.

"Neesh, are you good?" she whispered, refusing to turn away from the carnage.

"No. But we need to move on," he whimpered, wiping his regurgitate from his lips and proceeding to take a sip of his canteen. "Whatever did this, it's not human!" Nishfar continued. "The outcome of this fight. This result. It's feral, almost bestial, showing little to no emotion. It's either an animal, or something someone programmed to act like an animal."

As he spoke Cass reached down and wiped some human entrails off of a shirt, immediately a degree of fear took hold. The men that had been slaughtered in this hallway were not insurgents, the insignia on the soldiers shoulder pad identified him as F.H.A. Her heart sank. Nishfar turned around and noticed her immediate change in demeanour. "What is it Cass?" he questioned, his tone almost commanding.

"These are your brother's men and women!" she responded with dismay.

***

Nishfar now did well to hold his stomach having already thrown up three times, and that was just on the stair case leading into the maze of tunnels beneath the base. Much the same as the ones experienced by the Planetary News First drone, when it encountered Keifar nights before, these corridors were claustrophobically narrow. Add to that the fear inducing, gut wrenching, mutilated remains of those who had previously traversed this very path and the entire venture became a true test of one's mental fortitude.

Cass paid little heed to the lifeless remains as she slowly and methodically advanced forward, her Las-Carbine's under barrel fusion torch providing about forty feet of light in front of her. Further ahead of them she could hear scuttling, the kind that could only be rats darting and dashing in terror.

"Rats?" Nishfar whispered, his words carrying a little further than both he and Cass would have liked. "The little critters were once man's gift to foreign shores, now the little bastards became our gift to the stars. Oh how I loathe them!"

"Not the time!" Cass retorted, her tone quieter and with a consternate abruptness. Nishfar had only been seeking to ease the tension, for which she was indubitably aware, however his tone did little to that effect.

The pair had been walking for little over ten minutes, the sound of scuttling becoming pervasively heavy, when Cass felt two creatures move past her feet with haste. Shortly after, six more came, this time faster and less conscientious than their brethren. Both Cass and Nishfar stopped moving.

"WE'VE GOT A HORDE!" Cass yelled under her breath, slamming her back against the side of the corridor. Nishfar immediately followed suit, throwing his own back against the wall with a pained grimace. Rapidly, near one hundred or more rats made haste past them. Some scurried over their feet whilst others squirrelled halfway up their clothing, all before disappearing into the darkness beyond them. Both Nishfar and Cass were frozen in abstract unease, halfway between distaste and fear. In less than a minute the rats were gone, the sounds of their scuttling disappearing off into the darkness. Cass sighed in relief, taking a moment to collect herself.

"They're referred to as a Mischief," Nishfar instructed, himself relaxing for the briefest of moments. Cass looked at him disparagingly, to which Nishfar could only muster a superficial shrug. "You said Horde, it's a Mischief," he reiterated, an unrepentant smirk crossing his lips.

Cass proceeded on, letting her distaste for Nishfar's correction fade away almost as easily as she had adopted it. He fell into step behind her once more, adopting a similarly crouched gait, attempting to not seem as if he was using her for cover. At this point the bodies were beginning to peter out, with countless blood stains remaining. The corridor was now becoming all but silent, the scuttling of the rats having disappeared into the darkness behind them. Whereas fear should have continued to grip Nishfar's already fragile heart, or so he believed, he now found himself relaxing slightly. Cass on the other hand continued to remain apprehensive, her military training keeping her alert and at the ready. All of a sudden, a scream echoed down the hallway, followed by the bloodcurdling vocalisation of a gruesome demise. It was female, that much was horrifyingly obvious, and it sounded close. Nishfar's growing ease evaporated almost as instantly as the scream had reached his ears. Cass immediately picked up pace. She was ignorant of what she may be running into and instead fixed heavily on the possibility someone may need saving. Nishfar did not want to follow. His gut was telling him that whatever awaited them was not favourable. For the first time since the war had begun, even considering that which he had already experienced, Nishfar felt disturbingly aware of his own mortality.

Cass was running so hastily, and with little breathlessness, that Nishfar struggled to remain close to her. He was, unlike her, soon losing his breath due to a lack of pacing; that and the absence of hardened military training that Cass had received. Nevertheless the scholar maintained a reasonable distance. He could see her as she approached upon the opening from which they both surmised the scream must have originated. It was a well of sorts, a large circular room that led to a concrete grill nearly forty feet above them. The corridor opened up on to a walkway, beneath which was a pool of water that Nishfar estimated would have been at least ten feet deep. The walkway curved around the entire exterior of the room, with similar corridors leading off in each cardinal direction.

Roughly ten feet above the corridor opposite, Impaled on a metallic strut that protruded from the wall, there was a heavily wounded female soldier. Her uniform was that of the F.H.A. and her epaulette indicated she was a Lieutenant. Like a waterfall blood cascaded off the strut and into the pool below. Tears filled her eyes as she looked on in horror, feebly reaching out toward Cass and Nishfar. They both knew there was no saving her from such brutality. It took mere seconds for the woman to die, her arms falling limp as her life evaporated in the most visceral way. Cass' head dropped. Nishfar on the other hand found himself staring blankly at the deceased. "Cass," he whispered, "I know what did this!"

Nishfar began pacing, almost hysterically switching between rubbing his hair and nibbling on his nails. Cass looked at him in bewilderment, unsure whether he had finally broken or he was merely thinking.

"You OK?" she asked.

"Yes. I know what…or who…or what, did this!" He reiterated, continuing to pace backwards and forwards along the walkway. His eyes were a mixture of fear and loss, displaying a pain he had not yet truly come to terms with. That, coupled with his frenzied pacing and his apparent break from reality, made Cass realise.

"It was them wasn't it? The armoured warriors that killed your wife? The ones that attacked the camp," Cass questioned. "They did this!"

Nishfar kept pacing, his eyes darting back and forth, his one good arm erratically gesticulating. Cass had never seen him like this and it was beginning to worry her. Nishfar had never been the strong one out of the three of them. When they were kids, Keifar and Cass had always been the ones to pick him up when he fell, or to look out for him when the other children bullied him. That fragility had continued into adulthood, with him choosing the life of a scholar over anything even remotely risky. Then in the space of six months his entire world had been thrown asunder, and in the last few days he had borne witness to more horrors than any man should have to in his lifetime. Although she hoped he had not, she surmised he had broken. Letting her Las-Carbine fall by her side, Cass reached forward and grabbed Nishfar. Careful not to apply pressure to his shoulder wound, she pulled him in close and gave him a hug.

"Look at her shoulder. And around her waist. Those are grab marks that could only have been made by something of considerable strength," he posited, embracing her tightly in an attempt to stave off his break from reality. "The precision gunshot wounds to her left and right clavicles, and subsequent ones to her left and right tibia. All to disable yet not kill. This was not the work of human soldiers, this is the work of drones."

Cass lightly released Nishfar from her hug, her expression dejected. He looked her square in the eyes and he could see the realisation of a knowledge she had yet to reveal to him. Letting her go and taking a step back, his expression darkened.

"You knew they weren't human," he continued, his tone conveying a mixture of pain and disappointment. "You knew and you did not say."

"I suspected," she responded, her tone defiant, "I did not know. I suspected after the attack on the camp. All the wounds we treated, they were far too precise, calculated. Yes some of them could have theoretically been caused by a well-trained soldier, but ninety percent of them could not. Add to that the sophisticated weaponry employed by them. It was there for the world to see, we just didn't believe it!"

Nishfar kicked out in a rage, sending rubble crumbling down into the pool below. His heart began to race uncontrollably, his pain escalating into rage. He could not fathom how anyone could program a robot to perform such heinous acts. The 'Mars Non-Militarisation of Robotics Act of 2070', that the Sectors Alliance had implemented at the dawn of space colonialism, forbade such acts. Yet here they were facing a war in which the M.N.M.R.A. had been ignored.

"Humanity cannot be trusted with the stars for we will just repeat the same mistakes of our doomed Earth!" he whispered, his rage fizzling out into contempt. "The great historian, Michelle Doran, said that in twenty seventy two. Ten years later the first colonial ships left for the big dark. Centuries on, here we are…facing those same mistakes."

"The Systems Alliance won't stand for it," Cass interjected in an attempt to raise his spirits. "They'll enforce the M.N.M.R.A., by force if they have to."

"Don't you get it Cass?" Nishfar continued, looking at her, his expression the portrait of a dejected pessimist. "The use of force to remove force will only result in further force down the line. War begets war. Heck, Humanity is good at it, I suppose when you're good at something, why stop doing it?"

Cass was about to initiate a debate in an attempt to brighten Nishfar's spirits, when they heard an unsettling clank followed by the sound of metallic footsteps echoing from within the corridor opposite. Instinctively, Cass raised her Las-Carbine, a move that would later prove to her benefit. The electrical buzz of railguns brought Nishfar's fear hurtling back and he grabbed hold of Cass, pulling her to the floor. The walls around them erupted with dust and shrapnel as railgun fire ripped into them. Getting to her feet quicker than Nishfar had ever witnessed someone move, Cass grabbed him by the scruff of his shirt and pulled him to his own. The pair of them dashed toward the east corridor, railgun fire eating up the concrete and sandstone. Nipping at their heels.

Nishfar threw himself into the corridor with little care for the wound on his shoulder, something he knew he would later regret, but it was certainly more favourable than dying. Cass was right behind him, or so he thought. As he turned Cass was nowhere to be seen. Fear gripped his heart. Leaping to his feet, he threw his back to the wall and edged toward the opening, slowly peering his head around the corner. Lying prone about two feet away from the door with her Las Carbine pointing towards the incoming drones, Cass looked pained. Her eyes were filled with barely quelled angst as she steadied her aim towards the inevitable arrival of the black armoured drones. Nishfar could see her leg was badly hit, her armoured fatigues having absorbed a great deal of blood. It was clear she could not currently move. Taking a deep breath, he steadied himself and prepared to run out to get her. But just as he did so Las-Carbine fire struck the wall beside him. "Run!" Cass yelled. "Don't look back. Find your brother!" Nishfar could feel his heart breaking again, first his wife and now Cass, this couldn't happen. He stayed, steadying himself ready to move again but again Cass fired in his direction. "Don't make me shoot you!" she continued, a brave smile crossing her lips, "Go!"

Before Nishfar could decide otherwise, Cass unclasped a grenade from her belt and removed the firing pin. Instinct took over as Nishfar dived deeper into the corridor to avoid any blast. A deafening explosion erupted behind him, followed by the roaring sound of rock fall and collapsed dirt. As the dust settled Nishfar found himself shrouded in darkness, anxious, afraid and dolefully alone.

Chapter Seven

The rhythmic beep of a heart rate monitor and the pumping of a blood infuser resonated throughout the room. Nishfar slowly began to rouse from his unconscious state. The room was incredibly bright, so much so that his eyes struggled to open to their full extent. In the air, the faint aroma of surgical solutions and antiseptic overcame the senses. Nishfar feebly attempted to move his arms but he found his body weakened. Yet as he attempted to move his wounded arm, he felt no pain. With his other, he reached up to where the wound had once been and felt nothing, not even a bandage. The shock accelerated his rising, his eyes fighting harder against the bright light that surrounded him. He attempted to move his legs yet they did not want to listen. Sure enough his heart began to race, the rhythmic beep of the heart rate monitor quickening as it did.

"Nishfar!" a feminine voice called out. "Calm yourself. You're safe!" The voice was not familiar to Nishfar, in truth it carried an accent that suggested they weren't native to Hakon IV. The attempted reassurance did not settle Nishfar's nerves, the heart rate monitor broadcasting as much. His eyes were still attempting to adjust and he looked toward the direction of the voice, trying to ascertain who it was. The figure was most certainly female, though her face was obscured by a surgical mask. She wore scrubs not unlike the ones worn by Cass in the refugee camp and for the briefest of moments, Nishfar believed it was her. "Cass?" he called out, reaching towards the figure.

"I'm not Cass, I'm sorry, I don't know who she is." The figure responded, grabbing his hand and clenching it with a clinical affection. "We found you unconscious in the tunnels, our scouts brought you to safety," the female continued. "I'm Doctor Alliah Maronne. I've been responsible for your care."

"Where…am… I?" Nishfar asked, his voice broken and his breathing staggered, a result of his time spent unconscious. "How do you know my name?"

He attempted to sit up, but the weight of his fatigue was near paralysing and he could feel the remnants of the sedating drugs.

"You're safe, that's all you need to know at this time," she soothed, resting a caring hand upon his shoulder and applying a degree of pressure in order to lay him back down. "Save your strength, you lost a lot of blood. We're working hard to get you back on your feet."

"Am I a prisoner here?" Nishfar questioned. Considering everything he had been through and all he had borne witness to, it was not a leap of reasoning that he could be a prisoner.

"Far from it, you're an esteemed guest" she responded with a warm chuckle.

Dr Maronne maintained her hand on his shoulder, and lightly gripped with an understanding Nishfar would not expect were he a captive. As his heart began to calm and his mind began to relax, his faculties soon returned. He quickly surmised that Dr Maronne's personality, his treatment and the lack of restraints all suggested that he was indeed a guest. Having deduced as much, his heart rate finally returned to its resting beat.

"I…apologise," Nishfar responded, "I did not wish to infer you were my captor. My reaction was simply a result of the horrifying few days I have had. With all I have witnessed I am surprised that my mind has yet been gripped by madness!"

"No apology needed," Dr Maronne continued with a welcome smile, "War brings out the worst in everyone. Whether through fear or rage, the results are always the same."

"You speak from experience?" Nishfar questioned, intrigued by her cynical response.

"I've witnessed countless men, women and children die. I've seen people kill through fear, rage, sorrow and dejection," She said, her tone darkening. "Having witnessed these atrocities I knew there was only one thing I could do, I needed to help people… So I joined the F.H.A."

Nishfar froze, his eyes fixed firmly upon her. He had assumed he was back in the hands of the government, but that assumption had abruptly been put to bed.

"You're with the F.H.A?" Nishfar further questioned, his tone expectant. "Is this an F.H.A. facility?"

"Well done Sherlock Holmes, your deductive reasoning astounds me," she responded with a smirk.

"Yes. You are in an F.H.A. facility."

Dr Maronne's literary reference bought a much needed smile to Nishfar's war wearied lips, he welcomed the presence of another bookworm. "You've read Earth literature?" Nishfar continued, switching the subject away from the F.H.A.

"Most of my favourite books were written in the old world," she responded, with a friendly countenance.

"I very much enjoy the works of Sir Arthur Conan Doyle," Nishfar replied, his tone suggesting more than a passing excitement, "such superb characters wouldn't you say?"

"I couldn't agree more, he was a superb writer," Dr Maronne responded. "Now as much as I would love to stay and discuss the finer points of old world literature, I do have other patients to which I must attend. Get some rest. For when you're fit, there is someone who I suspect you'll wish to see very much."

***

Nishfar stared at the clinical white ceiling in dejected boredom. It had been nearly an hour since Dr Maronne had parted company to go on her rounds, leaving him alone. The room was hauntingly devoid of anything he could use for entertainment. Not even a months old Mag-Slate, a state of the art holovid magazine, lay in the near vicinity. He knew it was no doubt due to the fact the F.H.A. could not stay in one place for too long, especially considering the insurgents and their drone warriors were after them as well. But that did not stop him from being terribly bored.

Like a disinterested child he started playing with the digital input of his bed, requesting it to push him up and then down, backwards and then forwards. The mundane form of entertainment still brought a smile to his face, as for the briefest of moments he was able to forget all that had happened. But it was not to last. His mind jumped back to Cass, to the explosion in the tunnels and his last sight of her, leg bleeding out and unable to move. His eyes narrowed with sorrow, water beginning to pool within. Nishfar felt himself about to burst into tears, near inconsolable for those he had lost, when the familiar whoosh of the automatic door signalled someone was stepping in.

It was like he was seeing a ghost. Stood in the doorway, flanked by two heavily armed F.H.A. soldiers, was his brother Keifar. He was wearing the same silver aviator glasses he had always worn, the ones engraved with his name and given to him by Nishfar on his thirty first birthday. Three weeks before his supposed death. His hair was long but tied back into a top knot and he had grown a beard that near touched his chest. Unlike the last time Nishfar had seen him alive, in the flesh, Keifar's once jet black hair had greyed significantly. But despite this new appearance, Nishfar knew his brother when he saw him. As Cass had suggested when she referred to him as 'The Hawk', he was clearly the leader, the bars on his epaulette showing he held a general's rank. The pair stared at each other for a moment, Keifar folding his arms, a satisfied grin crossing his lips. Nishfar was unsure whether to be angry or relived that his brother was still alive. His emotions were going haywire, one moment feeling like he was about to cry and the next, wanting to leap up and smack his brother square in the face. Nishfar, quite simply, did not know how to react.

"Leave us!" Keifar commanded, his gritty, broken and gravel laden tone conveying years of conflict. The two soldiers that accompanied him nodded and exited the room with practiced military haste. Behind them the door quickly slid shut and no sooner had the recognisable click signalled it was closed did Keifar noticeably relax, unfolding his arms. "Well brother," he spoke, his tone more informal and yet still gravel laden. "Imagine my surprise when my scouts informed me they had found you here…on the frontline…of a war."

"You let me…let us…believe you were dead!" Nishfar interjected, his words filled with a betrayed venom. "Dad even identified you!"

"That, my brother, is a story for another time," Keifar responded, his tone more direct than before. He marched over toward the bed, Nishfar's eyes never deviating from him. Pulling up a metal stool, he sighed, "We haven't seen each other in near four years, and the first thing you want to do is argue with me."

"And whose fault is it that we haven't?" Nishfar continued, his tone conveying a sense of betrayal.

"It's mine Nishfar. It's mine!" Keifar shouted, his placid expression giving way to a bout of rage and he immediately stood, throwing his stool to the ground, "IS THAT WHAT YOU WANT TO HEAR? You want me to admit it's my fault, all of it. Well there you go!"

Nishfar looked at his brother with a mixture of distaste, anger and yet an endearing fondness.

"All I wanted, all I feel I deserve, is an apology!" Nishfar continued, his tone calmer and yet still displaying a stern candour.

"Then I am sorry, my brother," Keifar continued, his tone calmed, and his words direct. Silence fell over the room.

The two brothers stared at each other with a mixture of animosity and relief, for a moment that seemed like an eternity. Breaking the tense atmosphere, Keifar offered out his hand towards his brother, taking a step towards the bed. Nishfar paused momentarily, staring his older brother square in the eyes. Like he had always done when they were younger, Nishfar read him like a book and could see his older brother was sorry. Nishfar grabbed his brother's hand tightly, and pulled him closer. The pair shared a strong grip and an even firmer hug.

"I've missed you, my brother," Keifar said, his tone calm and filled with a cheerfulness he hadn't felt in a long while.

"I missed you too, Kei!"

The pair held their embrace for near five minutes, both of them unwilling to let go, their brotherly love proving stronger than steel. Eventually Nishfar began to release his grip. Keifar stood back up. Retrieving his stool from the floor, he pulled it in close to the bed and sat down upon it, removing his aviators. Laying them down upon the bedside cabinet, he chuckled. "You know, the only reminder of you and Dad were those glasses," he continued, a welcome gratitude in his tone. "I didn't know if I would ever see either of you again."

"Well I can't say the same," Nishfar responded, his voice as firm as stone. "As far as I was concerned, I would never see you again!"

"A hazard of my previous employment," Keifar replied dejectedly as he stared blankly into the distance.

"Your previous employment?" Nishfar questioned, raising an eyebrow. As far as he had known his brother was a Marine Gunnery Sergeant, who'd been involved in an industrial accident. However, he now deduced, from his brother's expression and turn of phrase, that there was more to it than met the eye. Keifar looked at his brother, gripping Nishfar's hand tightly in his own.

"As you have no doubt surmised, my death was a fabrication," Keifar answered, his head lowering. "A fabrication so I could undertake a deep cover assignment in the F.H.A."

Nishfar's heart nearly stopped, his eyes betraying his clear surprise.

"Are you telling me that, despite being the leader of the F.H.A, you're a spy?" Nishfar enquired, his tone lowered to a whisper, suspicious of who may be listening in. Keifar chuckled, a response that amazed his younger brother.

"Spy is so clandestine, my brother," Keifar responded, his tone displaying a degree of mirth. "I prefer Field Operative. And Field Operative in the past tense. When I joined the F.H.A I learned a lot of truths, truths you need to hear." Nishfar again attempted to sit upright but he was still lacking the strength to do so, Keifar laid a caring hand upon his brother's chest. "Rest my brother, I will tell you in due time. For now I am heading out into the field," he continued standing from his stool. "You're leaving me here?" Nishfar questioned, astonished his brother would leave so soon after being reunited.

"Yes," he bluntly replied, putting his aviators back on with a determined smirk. "After all. Someone needs to find Cass!"

***

Three days had passed before Nishfar was well enough to stand on his own. Dr Maronne had dedicated an incredibly large amount of time to assisting him, despite the relatively trivial wounds the severity of which was only compounded by mental fatigue. Nishfar had therefore hypothesised that her devotion to his recovery was less out of a sense of personal satisfaction and more to do with the orders of her commanding officer, his brother.

Despite the number of books he had been provided, including a number of real paper bound publications, a novelty in the modern age, Nishfar wanted to be able to walk around. Today was the first day he found himself fit enough to leave his hospital room. It was an event he had spent three days staring at a ceiling, dreaming of. Dr Maronne had seen to it that he had been provided with some clean fatigues and a plain, plaid shirt to match. Originally she had offered him F.H.A. colours, but Nishfar's distaste of all things military forbade him from wearing such clothes and so she honoured his wishes. Freshly showered and dressed, he walked out of the hospital room and came face to face with a soldier. Much to his surprise he was saluted and, respectfully, he attempted a salute back although it was clearly untrained and poorly executed. "Sir, I have been ordered to escort you at all times and to support you in the exploration of this, here, facility," the soldier dutifully spoke, his tone trained, precise and militaristic. Nishfar nodded, a perplexed smile crossing his lips. He did not want a minder, but something told him he had no way of ridding himself of one and thus he could only agree.

"Very well," he nodded. "Let's move out Corporal!"

The halls of the facility were nearly as narrow as the ones Nishfar and Cass had found themselves exploring underneath the settlement. However, unlike those corridors these ones were well lit by fusion lights embedded in the concrete ceiling. Spaced equidistant from each other, hospital rooms lined the hallway with their doors carrying the name of the incumbent. As Nishfar walked away from his own he glanced back and was surprised to find that unlike the others, his door did not contain his name. Instead it simply said, '*Patient A*'. Turning to the Corporal, he tapped the dutiful soldier on the shoulder and pointed towards the door.

"Why am I not named?" Nishfar questioned, genuinely unaware of the reasoning and, to his own surprise, a little aggrieved.

"For your security, sir," the Corporal responded, with respectful countenance. "The General only wanted select people made aware you were his brother. You can never know who may be watching. As they say, the O.P.A. is everywhere."

Nishfar paused for a moment. "Wait, are you telling me that the Office of Planetary Affairs is the enemy?" he questioned, clearly perplexed by the notion that a government operation that supposedly worked for the people could mean him harm.

"You mean you don't know?" the Corporal asked, his expression displaying genuine disbelief.

"Know what?" Nishfar responded, confirming the Corporal's incredulity.

"The President has considered us an enemy all along. If it wasn't for the General, we'd all be six feet under by now."

Walking further down the corridor, Nishfar found himself focusing somewhat single-mindedly on the notion that the President had hoodwinked not only the congress, but also the public. Pretending to offer the F.H.A. a way out whilst simultaneously seeking their eradication. If this was true then everything he had come to believe about the war would unravel before him. "Sir?" the Corporal asked, shaking Nishfar free of his crestfallen daydream. "Are you OK? You seem dazed."

"I'm fine Corporal, just fine," he said with a duplicitous grin. In truth he wasn't fine, he was far from it. His entire world was collapsing around him and it was taking all his strength to cling to whatever sanity remained in his broken heart. The Corporal was not easily beguiled by Nishfar's grin and he began to smile.

"Chin up," he commanded. "You're not the only one to have his world thrown into question."

"I deduced as much by the sizeable force my brother has amassed," Nishfar responded, gesticulating to the various corpsman and staff working furiously about the halls.

"He may not seem it, but your brother is a hero to these people," the Corporal continued as the pair walked through the hallways. "Most, if not all of them, were rescued by him when the attacks started happening."

"You mean he's been helping people since the night the sky turned red?" Nishfar questioned, pausing for a moment and looking the Corporal dead in the eyes.

"The night the sky turned red?" the Corporal asked, unsure of the event which Nishfar had identified. "Do you mean the First Night: Fire Fall?"

Nishfar had not once considered that different people would identify that night in different ways. Immediately he mentally chastised himself, lambasting his ignorance. He was a scholar, although in some ways he had forgotten this over the course of the last few weeks, and he needed to think as such; he needed to get his brain working again.

"So here you call it Fire Fall?" Nishfar questioned, continuing to walk.

"We do indeed sir," the Corporal responded with a chipper demeanour, falling into step behind him. "It's based on intel your own brother secured whilst rescuing survivors."

"My brother was in New Pavonis?" Nishfar continued, a degree of animosity in his tone. He had personally suffered greatly on that night. Alone, and without family or a way to contact the outside world, he had to walk nearly two hundred miles to escape the carnage. The things he witnessed, the despicable acts he watched people commit just to survive, would never be forgotten. To suddenly find out that his brother was there, and didn't seek him out, raised in him a disappointment that he did well to mask.

"How many people here are from New Pavonis?" Nishfar continued, the pair of them moving through a doorway into a wider corridor, an arrow designating it as the way toward the living quarters.

"No more than twenty," the Corporal answered with a disheartened sigh. "There were more, near fifty. All of them service men and women. But they've died since, fighting the Insurgents here in New Arsia."

"Where are the government forces the President promised?" Nishfar asked, disbelief in his eyes.

"Did you not hear me before?" the Corporal responded with a puzzled laugh. "The Government are the enemy. She hasn't ordered any ground troops yet because she is hoping the Insurgency will take us out first…so she doesn't have to. Problem is, as the General said before he left, she didn't count on us winning."

"My brother is winning?" Nishfar queried, somewhat shocked by the notion that his brother could be winning a war he was waging on two fronts.

"We're not losing," the Corporal responded. "That much is true. The General has done a lot for this movement, turning us from rebels and iconoclasts into a force for the people of Hakon

IV." Nishfar could tell from the Corporal's tone, and the way he spoke of his brother, that people had a great deal of respect for Keifar. It was a surreal feeling. The older brother he once knew: the man who brawled in bars and beat up bullies, who had been a philanderer and womaniser, the quintessential loveable scoundrel, had become a leader of men. It was a surprising turn of events. But to Nishfar it brought a degree of relief. Because with that much power at his disposal, surely Keifar could help get him off world with Mahira.

Nishfar and the Corporal walked through a large pair of double doors into a sizeable underground dome. Scattered throughout the spacious room were various bunk beds, sleeping bags and tents. It was just like the refugee camp on the outskirts of New Arsia, except this was more hygienic, with better food and healthcare. As the pair of them walked through the room, Nishfar was greeted by some and nodded to by others. It was a stark comparison to the horrors of the camp on the surface. As he walked amongst the various citizens he started to notice people he recognised from the first camp. Soon enough he realised that many of the people here were those that had called the previous refugee camp home. Nishfar stopped. "Where did all these people come from?" he asked, already suspecting the answer.

"A refugee camp on the outskirts of New Arsia, sir," the Corporal responded. "Two nights ago it was attacked by substantial Insurgent forces. The government hired mercenaries who decided they weren't paid enough to protect them and then left. If it wasn't for us, for the actions of your brother, they would all be dead. In truth, we wish we could have acted sooner."

"You did what you could. These people seem happier now, they feel safer. You can see it in their eyes," Nishfar replied, the warmth of feeling in the room bringing a much needed smile to his lips. Ahead of him a pair of voices called out, a man and a woman. Looking in their direction his heart sank. It was the parents of the little girl Cass and he had tried to save on that fateful night, he feared what they may say. After all, their reaction to his departing the camp on that morning was less than favourable. He approached them with cautious expectation, but to his surprise instead of sorrow he found happiness.

"You said to us that more volunteers would come," the father spoke, his words filled with a warmth Nishfar had not heard in many days.

"You said in the darkest of days, faith was all we had," the mother continued.

"And we had faith," the father interjected. "Then your brother came, with his men, and saved us from that camp. From the insurgents. He gave us a chance to bury our daughter."

"Thank you," the mother exclaimed, grabbing Nishfar's hand before he could act. "To both of you."

As Nishfar continued on through the camp he felt his spirits rising. In the shadow of war there was hope, a light his brother had provided. It proved to him that there was still some good in the world. But where this excursion through the facility had enlightened him, it had also raised within him a great many more questions. Questions he would want his brother to answer. "So where is the mighty hero?" Nishfar asked, turning to the Corporal as they reached the far side of the dome. Immediately he noticed the Corporal's forlorn expression. Apprehension took hold, although Nishfar tried his upmost to silence those doubts. "He has not returned from his excursion to find your friend, neither has his squad," the Corporal continued. "As per protocol, we are to wait another twenty four hours and, if we hear nothing by then, we're to activate article Three Sixteen."

Nishfar had always been suspicious of military protocols and government articles. All of them spoke of bureaucracy, of lies within lies shrouded in a veneer of more falsehoods. Layers upon layers of red tape that would ultimately result in someone or some group becoming disenfranchised, disassembled or worse, destroyed.

"I'm going to go out on a limb here and say that Three Sixteen is some form of evacuation protocol," Nishfar questioned. "But knowing my brother, it probably involves an element of destruction."

"I'm not permitted to discuss that with you sir," the Corporal replied with military astringency. "Ever the loyal soldier, aye Corporal," Nishfar contended with a despondent glare in his direction. "Can't break protocol, stars forbid. After all, you do work for the government... Oh wait, you're the resistance!"

Nishfar could no longer hide the disdain in his words, the Corporal feeling the full force of his venomous sarcasm.

"Look, sir, it's not about acting like the government, it's about following procedure. About sticking to one's rank," the Corporal responded, his expression filled with pride. "We use rank loosely here, looser than the Marines, Navy and even the Planetary Defence Force, but we still use it, and with rank comes protocol. It keeps the force moving, together and consistent! It keeps our hope alive!" Nishfar was caught off guard by the strength of the Corporals argument. He immediately realised the folly of his words and to the Corporal's credit, his sarcasm had been put to bed.

"My apologies, Corporal," Nishfar conceded, bowing his head in accord with his words. "It has been a tough few weeks and it appears to have affected my judgement."

"You needn't apologise sir," the Corporal continued with a humble smile. "You show the same passion as your brother."

Chapter Eight

Nishfar eagerly awaited news from his brother. He had been given dispensation to enter the command room, from where all F.H.A. operations were controlled and conducted. Like many of the operations staff, the Corporal who had become his security detail, and the officers on watch, he stared at the holo-display map of New Arsia with trepidation. At the top, a digital clock counted down the hours and minutes left until the initiation of protocol 'Three Sixteen'. There were fifteen minutes left.

Nishfar was sat on a chair not unlike his own back home, or at least the one he had before the devastation. Much like he did in his study, he sat on the chair backwards. Whereas at home he would look to the stars, now his eyes were fixed firmly on a ticking clock. A palpable silence filled the room, with information and commands being passed by subtle whisper rather than the usual assertive volume. Nishfar ignored all of it, preferring instead to quietly hum one of his favourite orchestral pieces: Canon in D major.

As the clock hit one minute, the officers in the room began a frenzied series of actions, darting between displays and issuing commands to their immediate subordinates. Nishfar could sense they were initiating 'Three Sixteen', but he could not help but feel it was premature. Since they were children, Keifar had always sought to make an entrance or some similarly grand gesture, seeking always to make memories rather than simply be in them. Nishfar found himself tightly clasping his hands together akin to a prayer, calling to the stars for this to be one of those occasions. As ten seconds remained it began to look like that gesture would not happen. Nishfar felt himself begin to well up. It looked like he had once again lost his brother, he had lost yet another he cared deeply about. He didn't think he could take anymore. When all hope seemed lost, he leapt up kicking his chair to the ground in frustration; then the holovid flashed red.

With one second left on the clock, a call was coming in. It was from the General.

"You son of a bitch," Nishfar yelled, not afraid to show the tears that had begun to flow, tears that were now of joy.

"Command, this is Asskicker, over," Keifar called out, although only static showed on the visual feed.

"General we read you, but we do not have visual, over," one of the many operations staff called out.

Soon after Dr Maronne entered the room.

"Keifar, this is Maronne. What is your situation? Over," she commanded, displaying an authority Nishfar had not expected of her. Whereas before she had worn the clinical white coat and scrubs of a medical professional she now wore the uniform of a soldier; her epaulette displaying her rank of Colonel.

"Colonel, we have sustained heavy casualties. Insurgent forces have grown two fold. Blackjacks are in heavy numbers. Request immediate Evac. Over," Keifar responded, the sounds of railgun fire reverberating in the background.

"What are Blackjacks?" Nishfar whispered to one of the operations staff sat near him.

"The black armoured drones," she responded. Nishfar's expression darkened. He knew them well. "General your request has been received. Romero airborne in five," Dr Maronne answered, with a sense of urgency. "Can you hold? Over."

"We'll do our best Colonel. Tell Romero, he flies fast, I'll owe him a beer!" Keifar responded, grunting as the sounds of fire intensified. "Also. Tell my brother. I found her. Over."

Nishfar's eyes brightened. Finally some good news. Unable to contain himself, he yelled out with glee. "I KNEW YOU WOULD!" he exclaimed, without due thought for process. His mood rubbed off on everyone in the room, smiles filling their previously tense expressions.

"Don't celebrate just yet," Keifar responded. "We're not out of the woods. Over."

"You will be General, you will be," Dr Maronne shouted. Immediately comms were cut, without warning, and the room returned to its frenetic state.

Nishfar jumped over the railings in an unusual display of athletic ability and came face to face with Dr Maronne. "I'm going with flight!" he yelled, using military terminology he wasn't used to.

"I can't permit you to do that," Dr Maronne positioned with command.

"But you also can't stop me," Nishfar replied.

**

Romero was frantically going through the pre-flight checks on the Galex G6 Shuttle. It was a streamlined atmospheric flyer, the preferred go-to transportation of the affluent and famous. However, with the arrival of the war, the F.H.A. had quickly moved to repurpose several of them for quick insertion and extraction. This was Romero's personal flyer, retrofitted with two fifty calibre machine turrets on her underbelly and completely devoid of seating bar those for the pilot and co-pilot. He had removed the safety catches from the rear access ramp, allowing quick descent in exchange for a slow retrieval; it meant troops could disembark under fire without the tenuous waiting of most other landers. Romero's famed mechanical team had also welded additional armour to its exterior, thanks to the additional weight allowance granted by removing the interior arrangement.

Romero was the fastest pilot on Keifar's staff. He had flown in the Marine air core at the same time Keifar was in the Marines, and had been Keifar's first choice lander pilot. When Keifar turned rebel, it was an easy decision for Romero to follow suit.

Nishfar leapt into the back, ran up and slid into the co-pilots seat, showing little regard for the words of the troops who tried to stop him.

"I'm coming, that's my brother and, by all accounts, my sister out there," he commanded, strapping himself in. "I refuse to allow you to tell me otherwise." Romero looked at him with a mixture of respect and humour.

"Son, you had me at 'my brother'," he responded with a chuckle.

"Son?" Nishfar retorted. "We're the same age!"

"I know son, I know," Romero said, frivolity in his tone. "Load 'em up," he continued, gesturing out the window.

With professionalism, six soldiers, including the Corporal, loaded into the back. With them they loaded an auto turret emplacement and, to Nishfar's wonderment, the former Planetary News First drone. Now it was painted in F.H.A. colours and it held it's self with a military bearing.

"You repurposed it?" Nishfar questioned, directing his query towards the Corporal he had come to know well over the last couple of days. The Corporal smiled, turning his attention toward the drone. "Havoc, thoughts?" he asked, resting a hand upon the drone's metallic back.

"I'd prefer not to be referred to as IT! My designation is Havoc. My purpose: to protect," the drone responded, its metallic face contorting into something resembling a smile. Nishfar's expression filled with both astonishment and a degree of delight. The Corporal's countenance brightened as well.

"You know your new role?" Nishfar questioned, astounded by the drone's change in personality. It had been surmised that AI could repurpose it's self with ease, after all artificial intelligence was tantamount to artificial sentience. But standard programming protocol, due to the Sectors Alliance's stringent laws on Artificial Intelligence, following the AI Wars of the late twenty first century, meant digital intellect had to contain various safe guards. One of those Safe Guards was programming any and all drones with a disability to evolve. It was clear, by Havoc's new persona, that whomever was responsible for his repurposing had temporarily eliminated these safe guards. It was something that was both illegal, but as Nishfar had slowly come to realise in the face of recent events, necessary.

"I indeed know my new role. I learned a lot as a reporter. But my purpose, my calling, is to protect people," Havoc responded, his digital modulation fluctuating akin to the human inflection of delight. "I have always believed my journalism did so. But now I realise that, as much as we may wish it so, words are not always powerful enough to protect. Where words fail, force prevails."

The huge bay doors above the shuttle opened up, revealing the towering trees of the local rainforest. In front of Nishfar the transporter's holovid display burst into life, Romero frantically gesticulating across the various read outs and confirming a variety of engine settings. Taking control of the flight stick, the hotshot pilot kicked the ignition peddle with force and the shuttle leapt hastily into the air, narrowly avoiding the barely open bay doors. Nishfar watched as Romero brought the shuttle into a low hover with a haste perfected over years of flying. As people had suggested when they spoke of him, he had more than a passing skill at flying. He was an ace. "There is no better feeling than getting a bird in the air," Romero spoke, with a distinct southern intonation that suggested he wasn't native to Hakon IV, "I live for these moments."

As the bay doors closed beneath them, Romero gestured for a map to open on the holovid display and immediately zoomed in on the co-ordinates of Keifar's field team.

"Nina, max speed set: three point four mach. control set: manual," he commanded, seemingly more relaxed than Nishfar currently felt.

"Certainly Romero," a female voice reverberated all around them. "Anything else?"

"Play that funky music!" Romero replied, a grin crossing his lips. Considering the importance of this run, Nishfar was surprised by the pilot's apparent lack of concern. He found himself tensing with a degree of distasteful rage, unsure how to react at Romero's blasé countenance. All about them music began to blare out. Boisterous, heavy guitar riffs pierced Nishfar's ears and caused him to grimace. Then the shuttle burst forwards with such haste that the g-force actuators took a second to kick in, giving Nishfar a brief feeling of being pushed heavily into his seat. The force so strong he nearly blacked out. Romero showed little to no response, his eyes fixed firmly on the sky ahead of him.

It wasn't long before Nishfar found himself clinging on for dear life as Romero ducked and weaved amongst the trees to avoid even the most sophisticated of radar technologies. With precision and skill, he threaded the shuttle through gaps Nishfar theorised it should never have cleared. Like threading cotton through the eye of a needle, Romero made haste toward the extraction zone. It took less than two minutes for them to come into line of sight, the battle unfolding around Keifar with horrifying ferocity. Nishfar's heart immediately sank. Romero slowed the shuttle to cruising speed, frantically gesticulating across the holovid display. "Nina. Release bay door." Romero commanded.

"Confirmed. Releasing bay door," the female V.I. replied with pre-programmed joy.

"Marines, prepare for drop. Zone hot," Romero yelled through the hatch to the crew compartment.

"Loud and clear," the Corporal answered with resolve. "Havoc, do your thing!!!"

"Yes brother!" Havoc responded with an animated expression and confident gesticulation.

The drone leapt up and out of the bay door. Switching from bi-pedal mode to flight mode almost as soon as his feet left the ramp. Due to its aero dynamic form Havoc was unaffected by the speed at which the shuttle was flying.

"Has he been active before?" Nishfar questioned the Corporal, pointing toward the departing drone.

"This ain't his first rodeo, if that's what you mean," the Corporal acknowledged with a smirk.

Romero brought the shuttle in towards the conflict zone with purpose, his eyes expressing a grim determination the pilot had not yet displayed. In that moment Nishfar realised that his previous estimation, based on Romero's blasé approach, was incorrect; the pilot clearly cared.

"Touchdown in 10, 9, 8, 7," Romero began to count.

"6, 5, 4…" the Corporal took over, motioning for his enlisted men to move toward the loading ramp.

The scene beneath them was carnage. Keifar and his remaining soldiers had held up in what had once been an apartment building in the affluent quarter of New Arsia. Naturally, due to the trials of war it had become a husk of its former self. Its walls battered and broken, its content looted and bodies of the deceased forsaken in the dust. Keifar was on the roof, four stories up, the sound of his Las-Rifle piercing the stentorian battle field. His squad was nursing three injured, not including Cass who was nowhere to be seen. Nishfar pushed himself out of his co-pilot seat to try and get a better look. He could not see her. Looking up to the shuttle, briefly noticing his brother, Keifar shared a look of relief. Nishfar smiled, putting the matter of Cass' absence to the back of his mind. Then, time seemingly froze. Nisfhar looked on with horrifying powerlessness as he witnessed his brother take a railgun shot clean through the chest. Keifar's body crashed to the ground, an expression of shock frozen upon his face.

Nishfar hyperventilated. Romero had put the shuttle into a sustained hover, releasing the controls in an attempt to comfort the man beside him. On the roof beneath them Keifar struggled to keep his own breath, a suitably savage hole in his chest. The Corporal, and his unit, moved into a defensive firing position around their injured general. With a frenetic haste, the corpsman attached to the unit dropped her medical bag and made haste to treat her General. Fighting against the pain and the breathlessness of a collapsed lung, Keifar grabbed the corpsman by the collar and pulled her closer.

"Get...her...out!" he whispered, before dropping back and staring to the sky. Almost exactly as he made his request, the roof access to the apartment block burst open and Cass came bundling through. Her leg was bound and splinted but she still moved with a determined haste, throwing herself to the ground beside Keifar.

Despite the feeling that the cabin around him was getting smaller and the metallic walls were closing in, as he watched his world thrown into disarray, Nishfar eventually calmed. Romero was speaking but Nishfar could not hear him, his mind drowning out everything but his staggered breathing. Without admonition, the scholar found himself uncoupling a seat restraint and moving into the cabin with haste. Romero reached out in a vain attempt to stop him but his grip wasn't enough to halt the determined pace. With no regard for his own safety Nishfar disembarked the shuttle, walking with purpose toward his downed brother. Making no attempt to duck or avoid fire, Nishfar's eyes glazed over, his spirit struck by a blow it could barely withstand.

Romero determined an immediate need for action. He turned back around and grabbed the stick.

With grim determination he yelled, "Nina, paint me some targets. We're going loud!"

"Confirmed. Turrets active. Acquiring targets," the VI responded.

Romero pulled steeply into the air, his holovid display bringing up a targeting window with a crisp visual representation of the battlefield below. Red boxes began appearing around targets. Instantly fear set in. Four of the painted targets were blackjacks, and they were attempting to roof hop in the direction of the apartment building.

"Nina, radio open: Corporal, you have four Blackjacks inbound. Engaging. Over," Romero said, the VI automatically opening a channel to the ground team.

"Confirmed. Preparing injured for extraction. Provide cover. Will radio when clear to go. Over," the Corporal replied through his helmet comm. Nishfar still marched toward his brother with a cold focus, showing no regard for his personal wellbeing. Railgun and conventional fire whistled past him as the insurgents and attached blackjacks identified him as a target. Noticing Nishfar approach, Cass gestured to one of the marines to grab him as she helped staunch Keifar's bleeding. Disregarding Cass' lack of authority, the private leapt up, grabbed Nishfar and threw him to the ground near his brother.

His arms caught the grit and dirt of the roof, grazing and bleeding with the impact. Nishfar didn't care. As the Corpsman and Cass worked furiously to save his brother's life, Nishfar grabbed him by the shoulders and stared deep into his eyes.

"Don't you fucking die!" he commanded, more furious than he had ever been before, caring little for the profanity in his usually amiable vocabulary. "You die, and so help me Stars…" he continued, a fury in his eyes that sought to block out the near unfathomable pain he felt in his heart. His mind flashed back to the day Layla died in his arms, the blood pooling at his feet and soaking into his clothes. Keifar lay before him, bleeding out in the same way and it was clearly fracturing Nishfar's already broken heart. "We're not letting him go!" the corpsman yelled, looking to Nishfar who did not meet her gaze. "We're not letting him go."

"It'll…take…more…than a railgun," Keifar struggled, coughing up blood and mustering enough energy to spit it out to the side of him. "I'm not dying here. Not like this!"

Everyone around him noticeably smiled. Adrenaline racing, the corpsman moved to grab the Medifoam and pass it to Cass. Nishfar's aspect did not change, a cold mixture of fear and anger in his expression.

"Mahira needs you Keifar, she needs her uncle!" He whispered between gritted teeth. "You. You are our only chance. You can't leave us. Not like this!"

Despite the excruciating pain he was feeling, his vision clouded by it, Keifar could see the determination in his brother's eyes. The furious, emotional, intent of a man who feared he would lose everything; it was enough to spur him on.

Romero opened fire on the blackjacks with a storm of metallic fury, his fifty calibre turrets filled with incendiary rounds eating dirt on their way towards their targets. The drones, now aware of the aerial threat now engaging them, ceased their rooftop hop and took up firing positions.

However, before two of them could secure a defensive stance, Romero tore them apart, their armoured shells exploding in a searing thousand degree hail of shrapnel. Almost instantaneously, the remaining blackjacks turned their rail-guns toward the sky and opened fire. The armoured hull of the shuttle absorbed most of the hits, but Romero was forced to cease fire and take evasive action when one of the shots shattered his visual display.

"Romero we're good to go, prepare for extraction. Over," the Corporal commanded via the comm.

"Confirm. Over," Romero replied with renewed zeal, pulling the shuttle into a steep side dive with full manual control.

Cass stuck the funnel of the medifoam into his chest, causing Keifar to grunt in agony. Releasing the cap, foam filled the wound and immediately Keifar's ability to withhold verbal vociferation ended. His scream of pain was almost deafening and Nishfar empathically felt his brother's agony, grimacing as he cried out.

"He has internal bleeding, the foam will hold, but he needs emergency care. Do you have a facility?" Cass asked the corpsman, frantically helping repack the bag,

"We have a facility!" the Corpsman replied, showing the nerves of a woman experiencing her first time in the field. Cass placed a comforting hand on the soldiers shoulder.

"You've helped save a man's life today. Be proud," she commanded, a faint smile briefly crossing her lips.

"We need to move. Drifter?" the Corporal interrupted, motioning for two of his other men to bring in the hover stretcher affectionately identified as a 'Drifter'.

With practiced haste and three men covering them with Las-Rifle fire, the group moved Keifar onto the stretcher.

Nishfar grabbed his brother's gun, and moved with him towards the shuttle. Making fleeting shots with her side arm,

Cass limped alongside them. Nonetheless as the group were about to reach the shuttle horror overcame all of them. Dropping down between them and the ramp, a Blackjack slammed into the concrete and turned its railgun toward Keifar. For the second time this day, Nishfar's perception of time began to slow. The contingent of soldiers covering them dropped to firing stances, levelling their Las-Rifles at the immediate threat. The electrical charge of the railgun increased. The sound piercing the already stentorian conflict. Putting her life on the line, the corpsman leapt in front of the stretcher, placing herself between the Blackjack and Keifar. The rookie's eyes narrowed and she gritted her teeth, expecting a painful demise. It never came. With a brutal avidity, Havoc dropped out of the air at near sixty miles per hour. Switching to bi-pedal mode as he did so he hit the roof with a force that cracked the ground. Both he and the blackjack broke through the concrete into the room below, landing in a heap on the ground. "The cavalry has arrived!" Havoc exclaimed, rising to his feet from within the cloud of rubble. "Move out, Corporal."

The Corporal could not help but chuckle for the briefest of moments, before the hail of enemy fire brought him back to the immediacy of conflict. Motioning the drifter to continue towards the shuttle, the unit moved once again with practiced efficiency, careful to avoid the newly created hole. Nishfar took Cass' arm around his shoulder in order to help her move faster. Once they were all on board, the Corporal motioned for the rest of his men to join them, covering the rest of Keifar's squad in their exit. All of whom had sustained injuries of varying severity.

Havoc continued engaging the blackjack in close combat, not allowing it to stand from its prone position. It furiously defended as Havoc tore into it with punch after punch. The blackjack feebly attempted to raise its railgun, aiming toward Havoc's midsection, but the repurposed AI was quick to realise his enemies' intent. Knocking the railgun to the side causing it to discharge aimlessly into the sky, Havoc proceeded to grapple the blackjack with both arms. Switching into flight mode he soared upward into the sky above with a blistering pace enough to shatter the sound barrier. Nishfar watched from the bay door as Havoc tore into the sky. Now suitably high, Havoc let go. The black armoured drone briefly continued upward before gravity took hold. Its rapid descent began.

"All yours Romero!" the Corporal called out, smacking the interior of the shuttle. Without pause, Romero raised the shuttle into the air closing the loading bay door as he did so. Nishfar hurriedly moved back into the co-pilot seat and was immediately made aware of the large hole in the window. As a result, Romero had now donned his flight helmet. It was a piece of equipment rarely used only in the event of a breach before or during high atmospheric flight. Nishfar was about to question why when Romero passed him a spare, the cockpit door sealing shut behind them.

"You sit up here you wear this, or you die!" Romero commanded abruptly, no longer displaying his previously jubilant persona. Nishfar secured himself in the seat without question, putting the flight helmet on. No sooner had he done so did he realise the reason. Romero kicked the shuttle into motion, accelerating to top speed. Physics took over and the view port exploded inward with horrifying momentum. Romero was covered in glass, some of which pierced his flight armour and yet the experienced pilot did not flinch. Nishfar looked on with a mixture of horror and respect before the g-force knocked him clean out. Romero had neglected to tell him the G-Force Actuators were out of action due to the breach.

***

Nishfar gradually regained consciousness, slowly regaining his focus. As his eyes came to, the outside of what had previously been the view port was grey. He realised they were back home. Beside him another corpsman, dressed in scrubs, tended to an injured Romero. He hissed and grimaced in pain as she removed bits of glass from his torso.

"Hey, sleeping beauty, you've finally awoken," Romero joked. "We thought you'd never wake up."

Nishfar groggily removed his helmet and shook his head, trying to settle his focus. "How long was I out?" he asked, rubbing his face with his hands.

"An hour, give or take!" Romero replied, patting him on the shoulder. The news brought Nishfar hurtling back to reality. He frantically clambered at his restraints, uncoupling them and making to stand up.

"I need to see my brother. Is he OK?" he questioned with a sense of urgency.

"He's fine son, he's in med-bay," Romero answered with a smile. "Tough son of a bitch."

Nishfar looked at Romero, unsure whether to be irritated by the remark or relieved. Deciding to respond with a degree of humour. He forced a smirk.

"My mum wasn't a bitch," he facetiously responded, leaving the cockpit in his wake. Romero chuckled as the scholar alighted but the corpsman quickly dispensed of his mirth with a sharp pull of shrapnel.

"You didn't say anything," the Corpsman continued, confident that Nishfar was out of earshot. "It's not my place to tell him. He needs to hear it from his own." Romero posited forlornly.

"Maybe," the Corpsman responded. "Maybe."

Chapter Nine

Layla entered the high class restaurant with a suitably dilettante air about her. Wearing a long, flowing red dress that hugged her curves and accentuated her assets, she was a picture of beauty. On this occasion, in a change from her usual hairstyle, she had secured her hair in a bun with a single curled lock hanging down in front of her eye. Make up emphasised her beauty, and brought out the emerald green allure of her eyes. Nishfar's heart began to race. Standing from the table for two at which he had awaited her, he took a step forwards to greet her. He was wearing a debonair cream suit with matching tie, his usually dishevelled face sporting a trimmed goatee. His eyes matched hers and in that moment he remembered why he loved her. Layla walked up, laid a kiss upon his cheek and then brushed past him as she moved to sit down, sending his hairs on end. Sighing contently, he turned to take a seat opposite her. Abruptly her face darkened, her previously alluring expression replaced by one of pain. She looked down as blood began to saturate her already red dress. Nishfar looked on, paralysed by fear and unable to do anything. Pushing against an invisible wall he reached out toward her, his hand slow to reach her. Sorrow filled her eyes. Tears of pain began to form. Her mouth fell open as she began to scream, yet no sound came out. Nishfar started to weep uncontrollably, pain surging through him like a forlorn tornado.

Nishfar hurtled back to the now with a shudder, his eyes startlingly quick to open. He was tracing his finger around the rim of the battered, aluminium cup that contained his poor quality, army ration tea. Due to muscle memory he'd been doing so for so long that it had gone cold. Nishfar did not care, his mind had dosed off from reality. He was still crying, a result of the torrent of emotions he had felt in his daydream and he made a feeble attempt to wipe away the tears. The mess hall in which he sat was empty, devoid of a single soul but his own. He was waiting patiently for news on his brother, since they had arrived back he had been on lock down, behind closed doors, going through all manner of medical procedures. Dr Maronne had been through when possible. To update Nishfar. But she was so fixated on saving the General that she was rarely anywhere but the operating theatre. When she wasn't, she was dishevelled, dripping with sweat and her eyes looked like those of a woman who'd never known sleep. Nishfar could not doubt her commitment to saving his brother's life, nor could he doubt the convictions of anyone in the facility. Everyone was counting on Keifar pulling through, and it proved to Nishfar just how much he meant to these people.

The familiar whoosh of the mess hall door broke the near silence of the cavernous room. With one walking aid, her leg now secured by a servo-splint, Cass limped in. Nishfar looked toward her and the pair shared a welcoming smile, although Cass' seemed somewhat dimmed. "How does he fair?" she questioned, her words colder than usual.

"Still no improvement. His wound is healing, but his spine, it's too early to say," Nishfar replied, staring directly at his tea cup as he did so. Taking a seat opposite him, Cass did not respond. She had an unusual air about her and Nishfar could not put his finger on it. "Can I get you a nice hot cup of this poor excuse for tea?" he asked, standing from his chair and trying to inject a little mirth into the conversation. He took a step towards her and placed his hand on hers as it rested upon her walking aid. She tensed, and her skin was clammy to the touch. On closer inspection he realised that sweat was dripping from her brow, although near imperceptibly so.

"Are you OK?" Nishfar questioned, trying to look her directly in the eyes but she would not meet his. He could see she was holding back a deep sorrow, her stare forlorn as she looked toward the ground without so much as an upward glance.

"Nishfar?" she began to question, her tone trembling. "Do you ever believe that we all have a purpose that cannot necessarily be understood by everyone?"

"I believe our purpose is defined by ourselves, and ourselves alone, it does not need to be understood by everyone. As long as we understand and accept it in ourselves that is all that matters."

Nishfar responded with an inquisitive look. "Why do you ask? Are you OK?"

"I have been deceitful," she continued.

Nishfar immediately paused, subconsciously taking a step back. Releasing his hand from hers and looking her square in the eye, he shook his head but a slight. If there was one thing he could not fathom, it was the deceit of those closest to him. It was something that he loathed and could never understand, yet of late it had become painfully frequent.

"By the stars, you know how much I despise deceit Cass. Why would you? What have you lied about?"

"I wasn't at the refugee camp to volunteer. I was on the hunt," she responded. Nishfar's puzzled expression continued as he looked at her, subconsciously taking a further step backward and edging into his seat once more. Cass' eyes finally matched his, displaying a near agonising emotional turmoil. It was the agony of a woman torn.

"I know, you told me. You told me the government were looking for my brother, and they had hired you to do it," he posited, with understanding, his aspect brightening. "That is not a deceit, you informed me, had you forgotten?"

Nishfar's face took on a suitably welcoming smile as he relaxed. But Cass did not relax with him and thus, almost instantaneously, the tension returned to his expression.

"Do you remember when we were children?" Cass continued, seemingly diverting the subject from its previous course, "When Keifar used to chase us off because we would pretend we were beings from the planet Earth, sent to retake the colonies?"

Nishfar noticeably smiled, his heart warming to the memory.

"I certainly do Cass, they are some of my only childhood memories, but they are the best," he said with a smile, "I always used to play the double agent, remember, the intelligent and manipulative one…which, for me, is far from the truth…well the manipulative part anyway. I always used to turn on Keifar in the end, and every time he never saw it coming."

The pair of them shared a warm chuckle, Cass turning her head and looking to the ceiling deep in thought. "I remember those days so clearly Neesh!" she continued, her expression taking a forlorn turn. "You and Keifar were my only friends, you were my brothers."

"We still are, Cass!" Nishfar exclaimed, once more reaching over to grab her hand. "You have done more than enough to earn that trust. Even after everything you told me at the refugee camp, we're family, and family make mistakes. Heck on that rooftop, you helped save Keifar's life. You saved mine in the tunnels."

A momentary silence fell over the pair of them, Nishfar staring directly towards Cass but she diverted her eyes once more. Nishfar gripped her hands tighter yet still she stared away. He could see the tears forming in her eyes before they had begun to roll down her cheeks. Nishfar could feel the emotion overflowing within her and in that moment he realised that she was holding something back. Reaching over the table, he took hold of her chin in his hand and turned her head towards him, matching his eyes with hers. Immediately empathy took over and he felt himself begin to well up like her. "Talk to me!" he pleaded, the pair of them now lamenting together. "After everything I have been through over the last few weeks, I feel I have earned your trust."

"But you won't want to hear of my conflict!" Cass responded, her words broken by her sorrow. "By the stars. I'm usually so strong, yet here I am, tears streaming, an emotional wreck."

"What is it Cass? Look you've got me crying as well!" Nishfar continued, the pair of them sharing a momentary chuckle. "I never cry… I'm so tough."

"Keep telling yourself that," she smiled. "But I still don't believe you want, nor need, hear my conflict. Especially considering what it concerns. My inner turmoil is little compared to the horror you have witnessed and the loss you have suffered."

"This is not a woe measuring contest, Cass!" Nishfar exclaimed, with a smirk. "It's about us being honest to each other."

"Then I need you to promise one thing," Cass said, "I need you to remain impartial, no matter what is said. Until the end. Then you can punch me if you want to."

Nishfar looked at her inquisitively. Why she would suggest a man, who was practically a pacifist, could hit her if he wanted to was perplexing at best, and worrying at worst. "I promise,"

Nishfar responded, although inside he worried that would not be the case. That scared him.

"Let me take you back to the roof evacuation," she continued, relieving her hands of his grip. "You remember I wasn't present when the shuttle arrived?"

"You weren't, you were inside the building. I assumed for cover," Nishfar responded, his eyes fixed firmly upon hers, giving her little room to look away.

"It wasn't for cover." She continued, apprehensively, "I was receiving a message."

Considering her words at the refugee camp, and the fact she was troubled, Nishfar's expression darkened. His level of trust in her was being tested. Deep down he wanted his faith in her to remain true, but suddenly for the first time since she began speaking he sensed a sinister air to her words. "Orders," she continued, "very specific ones at that. From the very top. From the President herself and agreed by the Congressional Defence Committee."

Nishfar noticeably froze. In that moment he knew there was only one order that would have her so torn, that would hurt her and trouble her as much as it had. Worse still, the Congressional Defence Committee was chaired by Daav'id; the man he had currently entrusted his daughter's safety too.

"What were the orders?" Nishfar questioned, his expression deadpan, his eyes betraying a growing distaste that bordered on incessant rage. He had been through too much over the past few weeks, a betrayal by someone so close was not something he wished to add to the list.

"Do you really need me to spell them out for you Neesh?" she questioned, her eyes pleading where her words were left wanting,

"Yes!" Nishfar responded, his tone dark, his expression darker still. Cass was noticeably browbeaten, despite her attempts to subdue the feeling.

"A kill order has been sanctioned against your brother. For acts of terrorism and betrayal of the sacred constitution of Hakon IV. All available assets must answer... I am an available asset." she continued, her words wracked by her pain. "Like you, when you were a boy, I am now the one that must turn on Keifar in the end. The one he will never see coming."

Nishfar just stared at her, a twitch in the corner of his eye, a snarl rippling from the corner of his lip. He was gritting his teeth so hard he could feel the pressure on his gums. Inside his thoughts were reeling, his mind darting between emotions: fear, rage and reason. Cass did not flinch, merely wiping away the tears in her eyes, trying to portray the strength of character she had learned in the marine core. "You...would...betray...everything!" Nishfar spat, doing his utmost to hold back the full force of his battered emotions, "All for a leader who has perpetrated a lie through her precious O.P.A."

"When I joined the marines, like your brother, I swore allegiance not to a person, or a place, but a planet," Cass responded, straightening herself in her chair as her warring emotions seemingly pieced themselves together. "Your brother broke that pledge, he tore down everything we stood for, to be a hero. But what has he done for the people of Hakon IV? Nothing. He has brought only more war and strife," she continued, a new found passion that spoke more of an attempt to convince herself. "These people here may care for him, but if he dies, some will fight, most will fall, all will return to their rightful place as citizens of our fair world. I don't like what I must do, but I made a promise that I would act in the best interest of Hakon IV, under direction of our Madam President. That was always my purpose!"

"Why are you telling me?" Nishfar whispered, his tone betraying a man whose world was finally breaking. In that moment, as the pair shared eye contact, Nishfar realised it could mean only one of two things.

"You're either telling me because you have changed your mind, and you wanted me to know the pain you went through with such inner conflict." he said, his expression giving way to a hint of morbid realisation. "Or you're telling me because you haven't changed your mind, and you have no intention of allowing me to leave this room."

Once more the tears formed in Cass' eyes, and Nishfar's heart sank. In that moment he knew his eldest friend would kill him.

***

All around him glowed the brightest, purest white. Nishfar could barely see his own appendages, let alone anything surrounding him. The air was cold on his bare skin, his body completely naked in an ivory world. His shoulder didn't hurt here, nor did any of his other limbs. He felt no fatigue, no aches or emotion, he was as placid as a still lake. Putting one foot in front of the other he began to move forward yet, as if underwater, an invisible force pushed against him. He felt both nowhere and everywhere, it was a peculiarity his mind could little comprehend; at first. But the brain of Nishfar Montiz was not so easily stifled. With lightning quick calculation, privileged by the lack of emotion and the clarity that came with it, he did not grieve for Layla, or fear for Mahira, he was simply present. "Is this death?" he questioned, his voice both echoing around him and yet remaining deathly silent, a fact that twisted the very fabric of his reality. "I am within my own mind, I must be," he surmised, his voice again breaking the laws of physics. "Then she killed me. I am no more."

His mind made a deduction at haste, using all the facts available to him and yet for something so traumatic his lack of emotion had him feel neither anger, sorrow nor regret.

As he walked forwards through the ivory world in which he now found himself, a place he deduced to be the very fabric of his conscious, he explored his own memories. His life, in snippets and flashes, passed before his very eyes. But behind every thought, every memory, a faint voice called out to him. At first he could not hear it, nor make out what it said, but in time it grew louder. With each increase in volume, its words became clearer. "Nishfar!" the voice called out, over and over again.

"I'm not losing you now," another voice followed.

The two voices continued in tandem, becoming increasingly stentorian. Nishfar continued to move forward through his memories. He soon felt himself drawn towards the voices, an unearthly strong pull on his conscious that eased the feeling of being underwater. Despite the memories that swirled all around, fading into the bright white world, he drew closer and closer to the voices. "We're getting something!" a further voice called out, this one different to the others.

"Come on Nishfar. Not now. Not today," the first voice called again, this time so loud it was almost deafening. In that moment Nishfar recognised it, it was Dr Maronne.

With a huge gasp of air, Nishfar shot up right, nearly head butting Dr Maronne in the process. She was with three corpsman, all carrying medical kits and in full field dress. As his vision came to, and his focus returned, so did the overwhelming, agonising, pain in his head and gut. "Lay back down Nishfar, lay back down," Dr Maronne requested, her words carrying an authority few could deny. "You've been shot three times. Twice in the gut, once in the head. Your head wound, luckily, deflected off your cranium, catching the inside of your ear and bouncing outward." she explained, carefully resting him back down on the stretcher he now lay on. "Whomever shot you, by the stars at least they weren't a good shot!"

Nishfar was dazed and confused, but dreadfully aware of whom had shot him. However his mind was drawn to the reasons he could still be alive. After all Cass had wanted him dead, she would not want a witness to her assassination, and like any good spook she needed to close loose ends before she completed her mission. Yet here he was, alive, after a superb shot had supposedly 'missed'. Regardless of the immense pain he was feeling, the morphine just kicking in, his mind began its lightening quick reasoning. Like security footage through a holovid, he rewound to the event as it took place. Through his mind's eye, in slow motion, he witnessed her level the silenced side arm with quick reflex. First she levelled at his chest, compressing the trigger twice and yet just before firing she aimed downward toward his gut. As he reeled in pain she levelled the gun toward his forehead, once more compressing the trigger and at that point it all went white. Yet here he was still very much alive. It was on purpose, he deduced, Cass had gambled on his life despite a need to maintain her cover, but why.

"KEIFAR!!!" he yelled, shooting upwards only to recoil in pain,

"She's after Keifar!!!"

"Calm down Nishfar!" Dr Maronne commanded. "You've been shot, and it's not a through and through. I have to remove those bullets. And considering we're on lock down, I don't have time to get you into surgery. So this is gonna hurt!"

One of the corpsman provided a plastic stick on which Nishfar could bite down. "I recommend you use it!" Dr Maronne further commanded, her bedside authority undeniable. "KEIFAR!" Nishfar yelled again, the pain influencing his volume. Before he could follow up the corpsman forced the stick into his mouth and Nishfar bit down begrudgingly.

The pain was agonising and it was all Nishfar's willpower to stay conscious. He bit down on the stick within his mouth so hard that his teeth practically pierced its hardened exterior. And that was just one bullet. The second one was deeper, that much Nishfar could tell from the focused grimace on Dr Maronne's face and the failed attempt to hide her empathic connection to his pain. With a scream from behind gritted teeth, sweat dripping from his brow, Nishfar braved the second bullet being removed. As he watched it leave his gut, he spat out the stick and looked directly to Dr Maronne. "Keifar?" he questioned, "Where is my brother, she is going to kill him! Stars be damned, she is going to kill him!"

"The assailant, how do you know?" Dr Maronne questioned, her expression showing she was none the wiser. In that moment Nishfar realised that she was unaware, as were the corpsman with her. They did not know Cass was his assailant.

"It's Cass!" he yelled. "She was given an order to kill Keifar. She accepted!"

Dr Maronne's face froze, her extremities following suit. Slowly she turned her head to Nishfar, her eyes conveying a mixture of shock and bewilderment. "Cass is the infiltrator? The enemy agent?" she questioned, dropping her medical tools. "We didn't know...she said she found you, and went off to protect your brother!"

"Radio them now!" he commanded, yelling through the agony. "She isn't going to protect him, she is going to kill him."

"Shit!" Dr Maronne exclaimed. "Base is on lock down. Communication channels jammed. We have no way of getting a message out!"

"Then patch me up. I have to get to him."

***

Klaxons were blaring all around the facility. The hallways were bathed in the flashing red hue of emergency lightning, all maglocks engaged to prevent easy traversal of the facility. Cass had not anticipated firearms discharge sensors, and those very sensors had engaged a base wide lock down. A medical team had been dispatched immediately to the mess hall. Considering the importance of the one person they knew was there, they were doubly hasty. This complicated matters for she had not laid a killing shot upon him in the hope that he would bleed out slowly, slow enough to be rescued later. The haste with which his rescue would now occur and the speed at which he would deduce she sought to save his life, meant she needed to get to Keifar and soon. If Nishfar made it there first her mission would be a failure and she would be resigned to plan B, a motion she knew would invite a great deal of collateral damage. There were women and children in this facility, not just soldiers, and she did not wish them ill. Ergo she had to kill Keifar as discreetly as possible; so that his death would sow the seed of doubt amongst a great deal of his supporters. She knew that many would remain loyal unto death, but most would see sense as she had and return to the government that sought the best future for all Hakon IV.

The main thoroughfare was blocked off, due to their Mag-locked hatchways closing and refusing access to Cass' hijacked code card. Using her training she had identified, with startling ease, a route through the maintenance tunnels and air conditioning vents. Both of which fed throughout the base and had no true lock down procedure thanks to the need for continuous oxygen supply. She had managed to rip an access panel off the wall in the mess hall corridor and enter into the maintenance tunnels from there; replacing the panel behind her. Like a shadow she disappeared from all surveillance, her focus fixed firmly upon her target. Tears still streamed from her face, betraying how much she cared for both Montiz brothers. But duty had taken first place, even when it necessitated a betrayal from which she knew her friendship to Nishfar would never recover.

She moved with professional discipline. Ducking and weaving amongst the maintenance tunnels with haste, fixed firmly on the location of Keifar's recovery room. He was submerged in a Medi-Tank, unable to move, which made him an easy target for assassination. Cass had already promised herself she would not make eye contact with her old friend, she knew she owed it to him to give him a quick death. Despite the immense emotional pain she could feel weighing down her heart, she was now committed to a course of action from which she could not return.

The maintenance panel leading into Keifar's recovery room clattered to the ground, the rattle echoing out through the empty halls of the medical facility. With all rooms on lock down, and all the Corpsman assisting with Nishfar or aiding the search, Cass knew she had plenty of time. She turned her sidearm on the tank with Keifar in it, her finger slowly applying pressure. "I'm sorry Keifar, but your death is our only hope." she whispered. Despite her stoic expression, the tears now came full force. It was clear, from the time it took her to put pressure on the trigger, she remained conflicted and yet somewhere in her heart she clearly believed this was what she had to do.

Suddenly the plasteel viewing window into the room burst inward, shattering into a million pieces like little more than glass. With steel stool brandished firmly in his hands, Nishfar barrelled through. Letting go of the stool, he piled into Cass' midsection with righteous fury grappling her tightly as he did so. The sidearm went off but the aim was not true, a bullet colliding with the metallic casing beside the medi-tank and ricocheting out into the hallway. The pair of them crashed to the tiled floor, their bodies sliding into the single medical supply cabinet. Its contents flew in all directions, falling to the floor with a loud clatter. The Corporal came barrelling through the window afterwards, his entry more controlled than Nishfar's. He froze for the briefest of seconds, unsure of how to respond to the scene that unfolded before him. The momentary lapse in awareness was to be his undoing. Cass broke free of Nishfar's grip for the briefest of moments, elbowing him square in the jaw as she did so, and levelled her gun at the Corporal. A suppressed gunshot reverberated around the room as his throat erupted with arterial spray, painting the wall crimson and sending him stumbling backward. Instantly overcome with pain and shock, the Corporal clutched at his bleeding throat as his body collapsed to the ground. Nishfar watched on powerlessly as the man he had come to call a friend collapsed, death ready to take him. Within,

Nishfar felt what it was truly like to live a nightmare. His eyes glazed over and rage took control. Before Cass could aim her gun once more toward the Medi-tank, Nishfar let out a bloodcurdling roar and leapt upon her like a rabid canine.

When the soldiers finally pulled him off Cass she was a barely identifiable, bloodied and broken mess. Nishfar had beaten her to within an inch of her life. Underneath his bloodied fists her breathing was staggered and her face was a grisly, broken visage that reflected how far this war had pushed him. All around Nishfar the world was spinning, his ears were ringing and his eyes struggled to focus as shock took hold. He looked down at his blood stained hands as the adrenaline began to dissipate, leaving behind only pain. "Mr Montiz?" a corpsman questioned, "Mr Montiz! Can you hear me?"

"Yeah…yes." he whimpered, coughing. "I'm OK…the Corporal?"

He pushed the corpsman to the side, seeking to see his friend. Other medical staff were frantically working to save his life, their actions valiantly fighting against growing futility. Next to his body another corpsman tended to the barely conscious Cass. In that moment Nishfar broke down, his eyes giving way to a torrent of emotion as tears streamed down his cheeks. He turned towards the tank in which his brother unconsciously floated, but his safety did little to relieve the overwhelming pain.

Nishfar stood slowly. He trudged past the two teams of medical staff working on the Corporal and Cass like an aimless zombie. He could hear the Corpsman calling out to him and yet he ignored it, stumbling out the door into the hallway beyond. He clenched at his gut, the blood of his barely stitched gunshot wounds seeping through his clothing. He showed no care. All around him medical staff moved with haste toward the room, carrying all manner of medical supplies. Flanking them a group of marines stormed in with their weapons at the ready, unsure of what they should do. As Nishfar trudged down the corridor several staff attempted to intercept him but their words couldn't rouse him from his catatonic state. His face was covered in the blood of another, someone he had once called a friend and now his heart lay shattered by her sudden betrayal. Reaching inside his pocket he retrieved a battered and crumpled photo of him, Layla and Mahira. Stroking his thumb across the creased surface, a drop of bloodied sweat falling onto Layla's brow. Nishfar tried his upmost to raise a smile. He could not. His will was broken, his soul crushed and in that moment he knew he could take no more. With Mahira first in his thoughts, Nishfar dropped to his knees and screamed from the bottom of his lungs. Through a torrent of pain, he cried out, burying his wounded head into his blood soaked hands, lamenting the hell that had unfolded.

Chapter Ten

It had been nigh on a week since the betrayal. Many feared Nishfar would never truly recover from the startling revelation and the events that proceeded it. Despite several attempts to elicit some form of response from him, Dr Maronne had failed. He just remained stowed away in his quarters, denying visitors, refusing nurses, barely eating and just staring at his photo of him, Layla and Mahira. The only news he had welcomed recently was that the Corporal, whom he had come to admire and respect, would narrowly make it through although he would never sound the same. Other members of the security team had made attempts to update him on the status of Cass, but he out right refused to engage any discussion in which she was concerned. Indeed he was so staunchly against discussing her that on more than one occasion he had verbally lambasted or physically removed marines, men and women who were just trying to do their jobs. Considering his frame of mind, people soon began to worry and Dr Maronne knew only one person could possibly get through to him.

The familiar whoosh of the door to his quarters reverberated around the room causing Nishfar to sigh, as he had done every time anyone came to see him. He'd become so enamoured by the whole affair that he didn't even bother to look in the direction of the door, until the person spoke. "I've heard you've been less than cordial with my men and women," Keifar said, his voice immediately warming Nishfar's heart.

"Keifar?" Nishfar exclaimed, leaping up from his position laid on the bed, only to grimace and grab his gut tightly.

Keifar chuckled. "Gunshot wounds'll do that my brother," he said, his tone carrying a brotherly sincerity.

"I never was cut out for war!" Nishfar responded through gritted teeth.

"I hear you saved my life?" Keifar asked, his body displaying a new and enhanced vigour. "Who knew the brains of the family would be my saviour. After all those years rescuing you from bullies, I guess I was due some kind of return!"

"You know who tried to kill you right?" Nishfar responded, showing little sign of relaxing from his sorrows and sidestepping his brothers patented yet historically accurate sarcasm.

"I know," Keifar replied morosely. "I know it was Cass."

"I don't understand how she could do such a thing!" Nishfar exclaimed, his words tinged with cold, hard resentment.

"Because Brother, war changes people," Keifar continued, stepping across the room and taking a seat beside his dejected brother. His newly augmented legs clunking as he continued to get used to their weight. "People you know, people you once knew, people you will come to know, war changes all of them. You should know the horrifying effects of conflict, you knew the true history of the wars of Earth. Do you recall the stories father told us?"

"The stories of how man knows one thing, and one thing only?" Nishfar responded.

"Destruction of his fellow man!" the pair of them answered simultaneously. Despite the bleak nature of the statement, the pair of them shared a momentary smile. Keifar giving his brother an affectionate slap on the knee like their father always had.

"But enough of the doom and gloom, I get far too much of that in the command room," Keifar exclaimed, putting his arm around his brothers shoulder. "Let's talk about something more exciting, upbeat, positive."

"Like what exactly?" Nishfar asked, raising an eyebrow towards his surprisingly light-hearted sibling.

"Well according to Dr Maronne, I am now sixty-eight point seven two percent machine," Keifar smirked, slapping his own leg this time, the impact more akin to steel upon steel. "Pure titanium, mined from Cogradus. Remember, the moon we used to go to when we were kids?"

"How could I forget it," Nishfar frowned, feigning distaste. "You always used to build tiny castles of metallic sand, then destroy them when I tried to help."

"I was a kid. You needed to learn the nature of things. Everything ends up destroyed!" Keifar responded, shrugging his shoulders.

"That's an incredibly pessimistic view for a child, brother," Nishfar said, with a shake of his head. "Even for you!"

"You're probably right. I can't remember my reasoning, I was a kid," Keifar laughed. "But then kids often do things without reasoning."

"Children, children often do things without reasoning," Nishfar interjected. "We were not goats."

"So," Keifar continued, braking the momentary laughter that had filled the room. "Before…well, before she attempted to kill me, Cass told me why you were looking for me."

"She did?" Nishfar queried, his expression displaying a degree of surprise. Her betrayal had hit him so hard that he could barely remember the friend she had once been. For her to engage his brother in a conversation on family when she could have easily killed him was perplexing.

"Why did she not kill you then?" Nishfar questioned, ignoring the point his brother had made.

"I don't know. And honestly, she'll probably never tell us," he sighed, dejection clouding his expression. "As I said. War changes people. She could have had orders to do it when she did and not before, she could have been conflicted, she could have been any number of things."

"The one thing she wasn't, was a friend!" Nishfar interrupted, his words filled with venomous disgust. Keifar rested a hand on his brother's shoulder and gripped tightly, staring him directly in the eyes.

"You're wrong brother," he responded. "She was a friend. Do not discount the years that came before that fateful event. The way she protected you through New Arsia, or how she led you to me."

"She did that because she had a mission to find you!" Nishfar said, his eyes filled with a degree of confusion. "How can you say she did that out of friendship?"

"Because, brother, she could have quite easily killed you once you had left the refugee camp. Heck she could have killed you in the refugee camp," he responded with righteous indignation, "for all we know she saved you from the blackjacks in those tunnels because she cared deeply!"

"What if they wounded her lightly, letting me get away so that she could then report back before you came to rescue her?" Nishfar responded, sounding a little more paranoid than his brother had known him to be.

"Listen to yourself!" Keifar exclaimed, grabbing Nishfar by both shoulders. "You're doubting everything! What happened to the brother I remember? The one who considered things logically, who thought things through, who deduced the most likely outcome."

"Like you said," Nishfar responded, "war changes people."

Keifar and Nishfar sat in silence, both contemplating those words. Keifar had feared the effects of this war on his brother from the moment he turned up at the facility, now he was seeing the result for himself. Nishfar on the other hand had witnessed horrors he would wish on no man. He witnessed what he had at the time believed to be the death of his brother, then the betrayal of a woman he had come to trust like family, and then was forced to see a man he had come to respect nearly lose his life. All this after witnessing his neighbours being burned alive on his lawn, a hand full of people fling themselves to their deaths from horrifying heights in the Arcology and the worst event of all, seeing his wife bleed to death in his arms. No matter how much he or Keifar wished for his old self to return, it was clear that was never going to happen.

"So the reason I'm here!" Nishfar continued, breaking the reticence. "The President has locked down the planet…but I need to get Mahira off world, get her away from this war and you're my only hope."

Keifar's head dropped, "How do you expect me to do that?" he responded despondently.

"You have resources, pull. Surely you can requisition one of your shuttles to take us off world." Nishfar continued, hope burning in his eyes. "We'd only need to get to the moon Cogradus, we can take refuge on Dad's ranch."

Keifar sighed, looking forlornly into his brothers eyes. In that moment Nishfar knew the answer wasn't good and his heart sank further still. A feat he no longer believed possible.

"You don't have any shuttles that can break atmosphere...do you?" Nishfar capitulated, his expression disheartened.

"The only vehicles the F.H.A. had access to, before the war, were civilian. All of them atmospheric," Keifar conceded. "We can barely afford to keep them in the air. If it wasn't for Romero's mechanical genius, many of them would be scrap by now."

Nishfar stood up with haste, turned towards the wall and lashed out, his bandaged fists connecting with the metal. He cried out in pain, a grimace breaking his sorrowful expression, "Fuck!" he crassly exclaimed caring little for his vulgar tongue. Keifar had never seen his brother this broken before, he genuinely didn't know what to do. "Neesh!" he yelled, standing and resting a hand upon his brother's upper back. "We'll figure out a way. The Montiz brothers always do!"

Before they could weather the moment, a flustered young operations officer entered the room, "Sir. You need to see this!" she exclaimed, struggling to catch her breath.

"What is it?" Keifar enquired with a sense of urgency.

"Terrorist attack sir! On the Soleri Arcology!"

Nishfar's world began to fall in on itself. All around him the walls became distorted like a hall of mirrors at a carnival. No matter where he looked his perceptions fluctuated. Like an automaton he began walking, swaying to the left and right as his sense of balance contended with this distorted view. Keifar called out but Nishfar could not make out his words. The operations officer attempted to place herself between Nishfar and the doorway, but he pushed her to the side like she was little more than a feather on the wind. The scholar's fears and anxieties were in over drive. Despite the immense size of the self-contained city, and the quite low odds of Mahira being a victim of the attacks, Nishfar still feared for his daughter. After all, taking into consideration all the facts, she was staying in the influential government sector of the Arcology and that would make the perfect target for a terrorist attack. Especially if that terrorist attack was orchestrated by the insurgents, under the clandestine command of the Office of Planetary Affairs.

Despite the dizzying fluctuations of the world around him, Nishfar's autopilot managed to keep him upright and moving in a forward direction; his mind racing over all manner of paranoid fears. Keifar quickly fell into step behind his brother. Caring little for the lambasting that could follow he slapped Nishfar across the rear of the head with the back of his hand, "Focus, my brother!" he commanded, displaying a stern authority more akin to their father.

"We don't know the facts yet, save your breakdown for then!" he continued. "But what if she..." Nishfar said, his focus returning.

"The facts!" Keifar interrupted with continued authority. "We ask no questions until we have our facts!"

The pair of them marched into the command room with equally testing expressions, both of which portrayed genuine concern. The large holovid display which had once presented a detailed real-time map of New Arsia was now awash with multiple smaller feeds. Each depicted the carnage unfolding at the Soleri Arcology, all first-hand views of the truly horrifying fear and pain at hand. One such feed, filmed by a Planetary News First drone, showed the garden district as a smouldering ruin. The once emerald-green grass pastures and beautiful oak trees reduced to blackened ash and burnt husks. Nishfar froze immediately. It was a reaction that did not escape his brother's perception, Keifar could see Nishfar recognised something. It was the park that Marie, his mother-in-law, always took Mahira to. She had taken her granddaughter there almost every day since Layla and Mahira had arrived in the Arcology, to play, to talk, and to watch the birds. The fact the attacks had included such an open and public place filled both brothers with dread, each for differing reasons.

"Pull screen three up to main!" Nishfar yelled, commanding one of the operations staff in front of him with an intense expression. The poor woman was unsure how to act given that Nishfar held no discernible rank, despite his relationship to his brother. Frantically she glanced around her for a superior, seeking permission to acknowledge him. Sure enough she caught eye line with her General, "Do as he says Corporal!" Keifar authorised with false calm. With ease the young woman gestured for the screen to take centre stage, enlarging it to fill the majority of the holovid display.

The Planetary News First drone, in bi-pedal mode, was slowly edging its way through the ruined landscape of the garden district. Occasionally its camera darted to the right or left, capturing the scenes of fear and panic as injured civilians scrambled for safety. Screams of sorrow, fear and pain reverberated throughout, piercing through the noise of the flames and falling rubble. Emergency staff arrived in droves, disembarking from their six-wheelers in a frantic effort to save lives. As the drone captured their faces it was evident many of them were holding back their own shock, subduing fears that would make them less capable to fulfil their role. Heaving large chunks of concrete and steel to the side in order to make its way through, the news drone did its best to move forward, its intent clearly to reach the epicentre of the blast. "Move! Tin-Man," one of the emergency support officers yelled, barging past the drone with little care for its presence, "this zone is on lock down. No press!"

"I have authorisation to be here, authorisation straight from the office of the Madam President," the journalist AI responded, raising an arm and presenting a holographic authorisation. The E.S.O. sighed, sheer contempt in his expression.

"Well if you have authorisation I can't bloody well make you leave but get in the way and inadvertently lead to the deaths of innocent civilians, I will shoot you myself!" the man responded with disdain. "This is why I didn't vote for her!"

"You and me both," Keifar acknowledged, a response that raised a subtle smirk in a few of his staff.

The drone ignored the sarcasm of the E.S.O. and continued moving through the ruins, slowly edging toward the epicentre. "The office of the President has informed us that she will be hosting a news conference momentarily," the drone spoke, its artificial tone feigning a degree of sympathy, "we here at Planetary News First have received information that suggests…bear with us, we are just confirming this information."

A pause followed as the drone heaved a large chunk of steel reinforced concrete to one side and revealed the bodies of a young family. Gasps filled the command room.

"We have received information that suggests the F.H.A. have claimed responsibility," the drone continued. "Peace be to the fallen."

"By the stars!" Keifar exclaimed, looking towards one of his staff. "Lance Corporal, get me any and all information you can on this attack. I need all my resources finding out who did this, because we certainly didn't!"

"Yes sir!" the Lance Corporal responded passionately, diving into his chair and furiously gesturing at the holovid in front of him. As his command room frantically began searching for the information he requested, Keifar watched on as the drone continued its slow progression through the rubble. With the help of some E.S.O's the drone heaved another large chunk of rubble to the side. Beyond he finally reached the epicentre of the destruction. As Keifar and Nishfar watched on in horror, the drone filmed a solitary child amongst a floor riddled with the bodies of the deceased. Blood covered corpses, some broken, maimed or beheaded, strewn about in a scene of utter carnage.

The command room paused, countless pairs of eyes fixated on the death. Many began to weep. Covered in a mixture of tears, dust and blood the solitary child wailed uncontrollably. Her screams pierced the devastation with petrifying vehemence. In her small arms she weakly cradled the lifeless body of an older woman. Nishfar recognised them both with forlorn despondency. "Viewers," the drone continued, moving slowly towards the child, "we witness the truly terrible avarice of these terrorists!"

Amongst the frenetic activity of the command room the Montiz brothers remained shock-stilled. "Keifar?" Dr Maronne called out from amongst the hustle and bustle, noticing his dispiritedness. "Are you OK?"

"Tell Romero to prep flight immediately!" he commanded, his words tinged with anguish, eyes transfixed by the carnage on view and the young girl amongst it.

"Very well General. May I ask why?" Dr Maronne questioned, quickly gesturing upon her personal holovid display.

"Because…" Nishfar interjected, his tone cold and devoid of emotion. "That's my daughter!"

***

Romero brought the shuttle into a holding pattern ten miles outside the Arcology. Even from that distance, the black smoke of the still raging fires could be seen billowing from the northern

111

and eastern sides of the gigantic, self-contained city. Keifar sat in the co-pilot's seat and the pair of them looked on with a mixture of sadness and regret. What once had been the shining light of the colony, the pinnacle of Hakon IV's success, now stood a scarred remnant of its former self. For Romero and Keifar what hurt the most was that the cause they stood for, the people they sought to protect and the purpose for which they had fought so valiantly had been blamed for the destruction. Worse still, the pair of them knew that the government influenced media machine, Planetary News First, would paint such a perfect picture of their betrayal that even the most sceptical citizen would see truth in their reasoning. From this moment on the war was no longer just between the government and the insurgents, it was between the people and the F.H.A. too. Keifar now no longer faced just one enemy but two. Forces that fought for the same person in spite of public perception, Madam President Roimata Aroha. To his begrudging acceptance Keifar had to acknowledge she had out played him.

"What's the plan?" Nishfar piped up, poking his head through the hatch into the cockpit. Romero looked at him with an unsure, unconvinced expression. Keifar shot his pilot an uncharacteristically disapproving glare, before turning his attention to his brother. "Taking the shuttle closer is a risk. Especially with the Arcology on lock down," Keifar responded, resting his arm on the command console, his posture deflated. "Those battlecruisers would swat us out of the sky like a fly, Neesh."

Nishfar's head dropped, and as it did, Romero turned his gaze back toward the Arcology. His eyes narrowed, his expression evidently pondering potential options. A brief moment of silence passed before he piped up. "I can do this," he interjected. "Nina and I, we can do this!"

"May I speak?" Nina piped up, "If anyone can do this, it's me and Romero."

Both Nishfar and Keifar looked at the command console with a mixture of surprise and respect. With an ego fuelled confidence Romero smiled at the both of them. "What Nina says, goes," he responded, turning and securing his restraining belts. "We can do this!"

"You heard the man," Keifar replied, tightening his own restraints. "They can do this!" Nishfar placed his hand on Romero's shoulder then patted twice, a thankful smile crossing his lips. "Thank you Romero," he whispered, with a nod.

"Don't thank me yet, thank me on the other side," Romero replied, gripping the control stick tightly. "Now strap yourself in, the party is about to start and the first track is a killer!!!"

"Poor choice of words!" Nina distastefully countered.

Five minutes passed in a flash as they flew toward the Arcology. "General!" Romero yelled. "Sensors are telling me the battle cruisers have identified us. We have to disembark soon or we'll be blown out of the sky." The combat klaxon sounded soon after. Keifar unclasped his restraints and stood up, steadying himself against the sides of the shuttle as he moved through the hatch toward the hold. Nishfar sat with his head down, eyes fixed firmly on his hands. He'd removed the bandages but the cuts and swelling still remained; a painful reminder of Cass' betrayal. "You won't have long to find her," Dr Maronne stated, resting a reassuring hand upon his upper arm, "once we drop in, Nina estimates you'll have fifteen minutes, maybe less, before we're detected."

"You can leave if you have to, but I'm not going until I have my daughter back," Nishfar responded with grim conviction.

"I wouldn't have it any other way," Keifar interjected. "I can promise you, we're not going anywhere until we have Mahira!"

"But sir!" Dr Maronne said with professional assuredness. "Our priority has to be you, the F.H.A. needs a leader!"

"With all due respect, Colonel," Keifar continued, noticing a rising distaste in his brothers expression. "Family is my priority. Therefore I'm sure you don't need me to point out that it is also the priority of the F.H.A."

Dr Maronne looked at him with a mixture of fading disapproval and respect.

"We are in a war with a government that cares little for the collateral damage it creates in this single minded pursuit of fiscal security," Keifar asserted with fierce conviction. "A government that is orchestrating a war against its self in order to obtain public support for the purchase of war machines and weaponry. All to rescue an economy they broke! If we don't look out for families, who else will? That starts with my own!"

There was a momentary standoff between the pair of them, their eyes fixed on each other, but Keifar's passion soon ignited a similar zeal within Dr Maronne. "If, for any reason I am caught or killed," Keifar continued. "The F.H.A. will have a perfectly good leader in yourself, Colonel. Everybody knows and understands that!"

"Turns out we have less time than I expected," Romero interrupted, yelling with an urgency he was not known for. "Hold on! I need to execute evasive manoeuvres and get us below the tree line!" Hastily Keifar dived toward the side of the cabin, grabbing hold of the nearby webbing, and luckily so. No sooner had he secured himself the shuttle executed a sharp, starboard dive. Romero brought the flyer below the tree line with precision, displaying the competency he was well known for. Once beneath the canopy the shuttle started executing rapid, agile turns, both port and starboard. The sound of the hull lightly kissing the trees on either side of it reverberated throughout the cabin. Despite this Nishfar remained apathetic, his mind fixed firmly on the safety of his daughter. "General?" Romero yelled.

"Yes Romero?" Keifar replied with a brief but tense hesitation.

"I firmly believe we should execute plan B. If I try to reach the balcony your brother requested I am about ninety eight percent sure I'm going to get us shot down," Romero said, his words teeming with unexpected doubt. "I'm good. But I am not that good!"

"With the Arcology locked down my only chance is that balcony!" Nishfar responded, his tone cold and his expression equally so. "We have no access from the highway, no access from the star-port, and definitely not through the government quarter."

"You heard the man," Keifar continued, giving a supportive nod to his brother. "The balcony is our only option."

"Very well," Romero easily conceded with a determined scowl. "I always did like a challenge. What's two percent anyway?"

The shuttle broke free of the rainforest just in front of the Arcology's main access highway. Where once thousands of vehicles would have been travelling in and out, the road was now at a congested stand still. Most people had abandoned their vehicles in favour of walking with their families, all seeking a chance at safety and all doing so in vain. They were fleeing the tide of war that drew ever closer to the capital and despite its vulnerability following an attack of its own, they all saw the Soleri Arcology as their best and only hope. Towering steel doors, meters thick, had closed upon the road leaving hundreds banging their hands against it with increasing futility. Around them several military and security personnel attempted in vain to turn them away. Tensions were growing to boiling point and a riot seemed inevitable. Romero flew towards the doors at pace, so close to the ground that it drew a trail of loose debris and belongings up behind it. At the last possible second he pulled vertical, all but skimming the doors and the subsequent sheer glass walls of the Arcology. The shuttle flew skyward, gaining height at pace. "Eyes on!" Romero yelled, his holovid display identifying the target landing zone with a large green box. "Prepare for drop!"

Romero levelled out just in time to come to a halt beside Layla's parent's balcony, hastily positioning the rear of the shuttle to its edge. The loading ramp dropped quickly, as was its design, crushing the balcony railing beneath its weight and sending metal plummeting to the road thousands of feet below. Unflinchingly, with a mixture of shock and grief in his expression, Daav'id sat at his balcony table. Nishfar took little time to leap off the loading ramp, Keifar and Dr Maronne following suit behind him with their Las-Carbines at the ready.

"Where is Mahira?" Nishfar yelled, his words tinged with venomous distaste. Daav'id had played a part in the attempted assassination of his brother but Nishfar did his upmost to put that to the back of his mind.

"In her room, mourning the loss of her grandmother," Daav'id acknowledged, his words filled with despondency as his eyes betrayed a strong sense of sorrow. "She witnessed it all, all the pain and suffering of an attack orchestrated by people working for your brother."

"You must be truly blind," Keifar interjected with anger, causing Nishfar to extend his arm across his brother's chest in a gesture for him to hold back,

"Either you are trying to lie Daav'id or you're being taken for a ride like the rest of us," Nishfar continued in his brother's stead, "either way, I feel very, very sorry for you."

"I'm not lying, your brother's men orchestrated the attack and you're too blind to see it, because he is your brother!" Daav'id said with vehement rage, leaping up from his chair and charging towards the group of them. "All of our intel points to him, all of it. It points to the F.H.A!"

"And where did that intel come from?" Keifar spat, Nishfar now physically having to stand between the pair of them lest his brother shoot. "Let me guess, the Office of Planetary Affairs?"

"Congratulations. You know our intelligence service, that means nothing Keifar Montiz, nothing!" Daav'id said angrily.

"Actually it means everything Daav'id," Nishfar yelled back, uncharacteristically grabbing his father-in-law by the scruff of the neck. "They're the true enemy, I should know, they've tried to kill me too."

Silence fell on the balcony for the briefest of moments. Daav'id's face darkening as his eyes betrayed the sudden stream of thoughts that rushed through his mind. Nishfar released his grip from his father-in-law's clothes but Daav'id's rage was so true, so tough, that it did little to sway his personal view.

"You can't take her, Nishfar. She's all I have left!" Daav'id continued, attempting to change the subject and divert the attention from his standoff with Keifar.

"She is my daughter, Daav'id," Nishfar responded, scant emotion in his words. "It is not safe here. You should be aware of that. After all, it is your beloved President causing all this, using a vote you played an important part in."

"You have no proof," Daav'id replied, shooting an abhorrent look toward Keifar, "as I said, your love for your brother has warped your mind."

Despite the rudeness that confronted him, Keifar did not respond, instead turning his attention away.

"I have no proof?" Nishfar retorted. "No proof? Those armoured warriors, the ones that killed your daughter, that tried to kill me. They're Drones. Drones in the employ of the insurgency!"

"Your brother's drones!" Daav'id interrupted, his words tinged with venom.

"No! The O.P.A's drones. This insurgency. All of it. It's the O.P.A." Nishfar spat, his expression clouded with rage. "Under the authorisation of the President. She wanted a war to kick start her failing economy. To distract the masses from the CATASTROPHIC failings of this fiscal year, her own CATASTROPHIC failings in office. My brother, his F.H.A., they aren't the bad guys here. It's you and your beloved government, if you can't see that, you are blind and I pity you."

"Folks we have to move!" Romero called over the radio, "I can't stay here undetected forever."

"He has a point, General," Dr Maronne interjected. "We need to get the girl and go!"

Keifar turned to his brother, placing a hand on his shoulder. Nishfar turned to him and nodded, before heading towards the balcony door. Daav'id quickly stood in his way. "I won't let you do this!" he commanded, his eyes fixed firmly upon Nishfar's. Without a moment's thought Nishfar grabbed him by the scruff of the neck again, threw him to the ground beside the door, hit the access panel, and walked inside. Keifar sauntered over to the downed politician and offered him a hand. Daav'id snarled in response. "I don't need your help!" he snapped, pulling himself to his feet,

"I guess common courtesy is all but lost on you!" Keifar responded, a sly smirk crossing his lips. "Never mind, you're coming with us nonetheless."

"I think not!" Daav'id protested, finally clambering to his feet and edging a slight backward.

"Trust me, Daav'id, I'm not too keen on the idea myself," Keifar continued, his expression showing little to no regard for the old man. "But my brother says he owes it to Layla and Mahira to keep you safe and so you're coming with us!"

Before Daav'id could protest further, which Keifar predicted was an inevitability, Dr Maronne walked up behind the politician and gave him a swift strike to the back of the head. Keifar noticeably flinched at the power with which the Colonel had struck the defenceless man. "Colonel I think choking him would have been more of a kindness!" Keifar said.

"We don't have time to mess around. He'll be fine anyway, after all, I am a doctor!" she responded with a sly smirk.

                              ***

Nishfar knocked thrice on Mahira's door, there was no answer. The excitement of seeing his daughter again was building and yet it was slightly muted by the events he knew she had witnessed and his fear for her feelings. He knocked a further three times and when there was no answer again he decided to activate the door panel anyway, the bedroom door sliding open with the familiar whoosh. Nishfar slowly edged in, tentatively awaiting a reaction he could not predict. Mahira was sat in front of her newly repaired window. In her right arm she held 'Ikle Paulie' tightly, whilst with her other arm she played with a group of small dolls. Nishfar's heart sank. His little girl, once so bright, happy and innocent, had been changed by war. The scene she was portraying with her toys was no longer the usual tea party but instead a recovery from an attack, and many of them were 'dead'.

"Mahira, sweetie?" Nishfar whispered, his tone carrying a paternal warmth. Mahira paused, but dared not look. She missed her father dearly, so much so that she had cried every night for him. Without her mother, she was lost and he was her only strength. As a child she'd been forced to grow up far too fast and with his return, Nishfar hoped she would have to no longer. "It's me, sweetie," he continued, edging slowly into the room and making his way around the bed, "Daddy's back." Mahira turned her head slightly, trying in vain not to look at him. It was as if she was too scared to look in his direction, too fearful that he may have been a figment of her imagination. "It's OK," Nishfar continued, lowering himself to the floor as he grew closer, carefully edging towards his daughter, "I'm back, Daddy's back, it's really me."

"Daddy?" she exclaimed, her sweet, innocent voice barely piercing the relative silence of the room. "The bad men came, they took Grandma like they took Mummy."

Her words cracked Nishfar's already broken heart and he was unable to control the tears of sorrow that came with.

"I know, sweetie, I know," he replied with despair, unable to hide his own negativity for the briefest of moments. Mahira picked up on it, burying her head into his chest and grabbing him tightly. "Grandma and Mummy are in a better place now,

                              118

amongst the stars," he continued, hugging her tighter than he had ever hugged her before. "They're safe."

"What about me Daddy?" Mahira said, her wide eyes looking up to him, lamenting his words.

"That's why I am here sweetie," he responded with a warm smile. "We're going to get you somewhere safe."

"We?" Mahira questioned with an expectant smile.

"Me and your Uncle Keifar!"

Nishfar stood up and grabbed Mahira's Mega-Cat bag from the wall, throwing it on to her bed and immediately moving towards her drawers to pack some clothes. Faster than her father, and now brimming with a degree of excitement, Mahira ran to her wardrobe and began grabbing her own. "We can't take much, sweetie," Nishfar commanded whilst packing some of her night clothes, "we'll have to buy you more when we get to safety."

"Where is 'safety'?" Mahira asked, her eyes expectant of an answer,

"Grandad Rin's, on Cogradus," Nishfar answered with a smile, "you remember, with the elk and the grey plains."

"I don't remember Daddy, I've never been there!" Mahira exclaimed, raising her hands and shrugging her shoulders.

"You have been," Nishfar smiled, recalling the day he took Layla and Mahira there when she was no more than sixteen months, "you just don't remember because you were a baby."

"A BABY?" Mahira exclaimed, rolling her eyes and shrugging her shoulders again. Nishfar could only smile in response. Despite the pain and suffering she had witnessed, losing her grandmother right before her eyes and struggling without a mother, she remained as sassy and loquacious as she had always been; her brightness lit up the room.

"Yes, a baby!" Nishfar responded, suitably mimicking her cheeky personality. "You were one of those once!"

"I know!" she yelled, slapping her hands on her hips, her eyes wide and her mouth agape with surprise, "but how did you expect me to remember that!"

Nishfar began chuckling. His daughter had him there, and he loved that. He had missed her light amongst the darkness of this war. Even more so, he had missed her correcting him when he believed he was most certainly right. Especially when he definitely was wrong. "You got me there." he exclaimed, grabbing her and beginning to tickle, giggling reverberating throughout the room, "You got me there!"

Keifar burst into the room, careful to hide his Las-Carbine over his shoulder. Noticing her uncle, Mahira leapt into his arms which forced a suitably quick reaction. "Grandad Rin told me you had gone to the stars?" she questioned, hugging him so tightly he nearly lost his breath.

"Well sometimes Grandad is wrong," Keifar exclaimed with a smile, a grin that could only be a result of her affection. "I couldn't leave my favourite niece behind with her daddy could I!"

"I'm your only niece!" Mahira exclaimed, pulling back and looking Keifar directly in his eyes,

"Exactly, my favourite," he responded with an impish grin.

The exchange further warmed Nishfar. Amongst the pain he had suffered of late by losing his wife, nearly losing his brother and being betrayed by a woman he called a sister, Nishfar had entered a very bleak place. Mahira and Keifar were drawing him back toward the light. They were the only true family he had left. "We have a go bag for Mahira!" Nishfar interrupted, raising the Mega-Cat bag towards his brother,

"Go bag?" Keifar chuckled. "When did you become so military?"

"I've been around you too long!" Nishfar responded with a smirk, chucking the bag in his brother's direction. With Mahira in one arm, Keifar still easily caught the Mega-Cat bag and slung it over his shoulder. "You still like Mega-Cat?" he asked his niece, as Nishfar grabbed 'Ikle Paulie' from the floor.

"Of course I do. Mega-Cat saves all the peoples!" Mahira responded with glee,

"Come on Uncle Keifar, you should know that," Nishfar interrupted sarcastically, "what's not to love about a cat the size of a small horse, that saves children from the evils of space monkeys!"

"Well when Daddy puts it like that," Keifar responded, looking to Mahira, "I know why you still love Mega-Cat!"

Nishfar and Keifar both walked down the stairs together, Mahira sat upon Keifar's shoulders. The three of them sharing a moment of laughter, the result of one of Keifar's aptly named Dad jokes.

But the moment was short lived. Dr Maronne came rushing into the hallway, flustered and near out of breath. The tip of her Las-Carbine was orange hot, steam rolling off. It had just been fired. Nishfar clocked it immediately and his heart began to race, he knew something was amiss. "Update, Colonel?" Keifar commanded, lowering Mahira from his shoulders and motioning for her to stand with her father.

"Blackjacks sir, on the balcony. All the balconies," she exclaimed, trying to catch her breath, "Keifar, it's a second attack. Mahira, your family, Daav'id, I think it was a trap… The O.P.A., they've got us!"

Keifar released the power pack on his carbine, checked the power read out and then replaced it with practiced military precision. "Romero, Colonel?" Keifar continued, his eyes ordering Dr Maronne to choose her words carefully,

"At this point sir, I'd have to say M.I.A.," she responded, fighting back her own fears. "The Blackjack scored a direct hit, last radio announcement was he was unconscious and Nina was bracing for impact!"

Nishfar looked at the pair of them as they conversed, noticing their tense body language and the doubt in his brothers eyes. Keifar would never openly show it to those under his command but Nishfar knew his brother well and he could read him like a book. "Where is Daav'id?" Nishfar piped up, looking to Dr Maronne for an immediate answer.

"He was in the shuttle…" she responded, trying not to match eye-line with Mahira lest she upset her more. "I just don't know!"

"Exactly, we don't know, which means they're fine until we find out otherwise," Nishfar continued with an intense determination that immediately rubbed off on both his brother and Dr Maronne. His countenance had the desired effect with Mahira remaining positive in his arms, a smile never leaving her expression.

"Mahira, darling, you need to stay close to Daddy. DO NOT leave my side," Nishfar commanded with paternal authority, crouching in order to be on the level with her. "If you can't see me, you call for Keifar, OK?"

"OK, Daddy," she responded with an acknowledging nod.

"You sound like you have a plan brewing brother?" Keifar questioned, the sounds of gunfire and railgun charges becoming increasingly audible.

"We make for the University," Nishfar answered with authority. "I still have access to Layla's credentials. The Aerospace and Aeronautics department have a seven strong fleet of Galex H.S.L.A. Science Boats. We can use one to escape!"

"H.S.L.A?" Dr Maronne questioned, her expression signalling she was most certainly unaware of the meaning.

"High Speed, Low Atmosphere," Keifar responded. "Essentially, they're skimmers, but they'll fly up to around two thousand feet. It's enough to get us back to base."

"Flying them is a piece of cake," Nishfar continued, "Dad used to take me and Keifar out in them all the time."

"I used to crash them...a lot," Keifar responded with a shrug.

"That's why I will fly," Nishfar responded. "Leaves you free to shoot the bad guys."

***

Keifar, Dr Maronne, Nishfar and Mahira all edged into Daav'id's garage slowly and quietly. Outside the sounds of battle were intensifying and they could only surmise that Arcology security staff were losing. After all they lacked the resources to take on such heavily armed, heavily armoured foes as the Blackjacks. The O.P.A. had no doubt counted on that. Under a sheet of tarpaulin covered in a faint layer of dust sat a vintage Harmony Argo B632 Cleopatra. It was one of the first six wheeler, full-fusion, vehicles ever produced and had turned the once small family business of Harmony Argo into the massive, multi-colony, corporation it was today. Nishfar and Daav'id had been working on it together, over the past four years, at the behest of Layla who decided they should share a hobby when they were both in town. Much to Nishfar's annoyance, Daav'id knew very little about engineering, let alone vehicles. As a result Nishfar did most of the work. Despite engineering being the field in which Layla had excelled, Nishfar had done a superb job from reading countless books on the subject matter.

As he whipped the tarpaulin off, the cloud of dust rising in the air and darting away with the gust that followed, Keifar looked on in amazement. "A Cleopatra?" he exclaimed, tracing his hand lightly across her exterior and walking around her, his eyes teeming with admiration. "You restored this?"

"Well, me and Daav'id!" Nishfar responded, his tone suitably darkening at his father-in-law's name. "But mostly me. It was mainly Daav'id's money."

"Grandad doesn't know anything about vehicles, like Daddy does!" Mahira piped up in staunch defence of her father, words that brought a smile to everyone.

Nishfar placed a caring hand on his daughter's head, conveying a paternal warmth. "I'm guessing she runs?" Keifar continued.

"Of course she runs," Nishfar exclaimed, his expression betraying contempt for the perceived insult. Keifar immediately took a step back, raising his arms in a gesture of reparation. "Should never have doubted you, my brother!" he responded. "Can I drive?"

Nishfar thought on the question for a moment. Ever since he had begun restoring the Cleopatra he had dreamed of being the first one to drive her. However, he needed to make sure Mahira was safe and the best way to do that would be to sit with her in the back. "It pains me, but yes you can!" Nishfar replied, lowering his head.

"Are you boys done being boys?" Dr Maronne asked with a smirk. "Because we need to get out of here, Blackjacks are drawing in."

"Sally. Unlock. Code four seven echo golf delta," Nishfar called out, eyes fixed firmly on Dr Maronne, an impish grin of his own across his lips. The sound of locking mechanisms unhinging reverberated throughout the garage and then all six doors to the vehicle opened upward and over. "Your carriage awaits," Keifar beamed with enthusiasm, gesturing for Dr Maronne to get in to the front passenger seat,

"You're so romantic!" she sarcastically responded, brushing past him and edging into the seat. It was in that briefest of moments that Nishfar finally clicked. Their relationship was more than just friendship and camaraderie, they were romantically attached. Internally he lambasted himself, he should have known.

Chapter Eleven

The Harmony Argo B632 Cleopatra smashed through the front plate glass windows of the university entrance foyer. Keifar slammed his foot on the breaks, Nishfar bracing himself over Mahira to protect her from any potential impact. The vintage six wheeler skidded left, then right, as Keifar wrestled with the controlled steering in a somewhat vein attempt to limit the external damage. The reception desk exploded outward in a hail of wooden splinters and computer parts as they smashed through it. The electronic double doors behind it shot open automatically mere seconds before the vehicle impacted, but it was barely wide enough to fit the six wheeler. Both sides ground against the door frame with a sickening squeal. The corridor beyond was a slight wider and thanks to the door the six wheeler had slowed considerably, but it was still moving at pace. Nevertheless Keifar had now managed to wrestle control and was able to maintain a reasonably straight line. "They still on us!" he cried out, eyes fixed firmly upon the corridor in front of him. "Tell me they're not still on us!"

"I can't see them," Dr Maronne yelled, "think you threw them off."

"Here's to hoping," Nishfar piped up, holding Mahira tight to his chest.

The Cleopatra crashed through the doorway at the furthest end of the corridor and ground to a halt against the dry wall beyond it, dust and mortar crumbling down upon the bonnet. Sweat was dripping from Keifar's brow, his undershirt all but drenched and his breathing, heavy; but they were alive. "We need to move!" Dr Maronne commanded, kicking open the six-wheelers rear hatch and hopping out. Instinctively, she took up a covering position, kneeling with her Las-Carbine pointing down the hallway, eyes narrowed in focus. Nishfar released Mahira from his grip and shot a comforting smile in her direction, she responded with a faint smile of her own. "You OK?" he whispered. "Because your Uncle's driving leaves a lot to be desired!".

"Hey!" Keifar responded, feigning disgust. Mahira could only laugh, her childish mirth enough to calm even the tensest moment.

"We really need to move," Dr Maronne piped up. Before Nishfar or Keifar could respond the dread inducing sound of railgun fire filled the corridor. The Harmony Argo's rear hatch was peppered with impact burns as shots collided with it. Nishfar popped his head over the seat to get a look at their assailants. Immediately he tensed. Keifar leapt out of the driver's seat and, with pace, opened Mahira's door. Noticing his brother's body language, Nishfar paused, "What's up brother?"

"They know I'm here," Keifar responded with concern.

"Maronne thought it may have been a trap," Nishfar responded, his tone matching his brother's concern,

"I hate to say I'm right but we've got four blackjacks on us, not one, not two, four," Dr Maronne interjected as she threw herself over the roof and crashed to the ground by Keifar's feet.

"Only one reason they'd hunt us with such numbers," Keifar continued. "Their commander knows an asset is in play."

"You," Nishfar replied dejectedly. "It was all a trap!"

The group hastily ran down the corridor toward the science department. Nishfar had Mahira in his arms and tucked into his chest, positioning himself between Keifar and Maronne as she covered their escape. An explosion rocked the building as the fusion reactor in the B632 Cleopatra went up under sustained fire, nearly knocking them from their feet. Dr Maronne couldn't see any assailants in her line of fire, but she knew that wouldn't be for long. With little care for the automatic door Keifar smashed through with his shoulder. The whole entryway collapsed inward and collided with the metallic floor beyond as he rushed over it. "The hanger is the fourth door on the right," Nishfar yelled. "Our activation code is Dr Montiz, Echo, Bravo, Charlie, Zebra, Zero, Zero, Six, Four!"

"That's a mouthful," Keifar jested,

"I didn't design the security," Nishfar responded with a similar degree of mirth.

"Would you boys quit it, I'd rather not die thanks to your attempts at humour," Dr Maronne interjected with a stern look, forcing impudent expressions from both brothers. Mahira, entertained by the whole affair and distracted from the imminent threat, held her hand up to high five Dr Maronne who responded in kind.

Entering the hanger, the trio were relieved to find one of the H.S.L.A. boats remained intact and ready for launch. Another sat beside it with its belly open and mechanical entrails strewn across the hanger floor whilst the rest were nowhere to be seen. The entire hangar spoke of the haste with which the students vacated the university when the attack began, the bags and coats that remained a testament to the speed at which they left. Nishfar let Mahira down from his back and signalled for her to stand near her uncle whilst he moved up toward the skimmer. Keifar took Mahira under his arm and then checked his Las-Carbine was loaded as Dr Maronne positioned herself at the door. She took a knee and aimed her own carbine down the hall, ready for the inevitable. Her breathing was staggered and sweat now dripped from her brow, anxious at what would soon round the corner.

Nishfar pulled the door release handle on the H.S.L.A and hopped into the hatch, choosing not to wait for the ladder to lower. "Activation Code: Doctor Montiz. Echo. Bravo. Charlie. Zebra. Zero. Zero. Six. Four!" Nishfar commanded, leaping into the pilot seat and adjusting it to match his size. "Computer confirm. Activation Doctor Montiz," the skimmer responded with a digital, yet feminine, vocalisation. "Have you got a cold?"

"What?" Nishfar posited, confused by the virtual intelligence.

"Your voice is deeper than usual Dr Montiz," the skimmer responded. Nishfar believed in that moment that, if it had a face, it would be sharing a sly smile.

Dr Maronne could hear the clunk of metal upon metal from down the hall and her trigger finger tensed as a result. Behind her, Keifar loaded Mahira into the back of the skimmer before moving to the hanger door's manual release handle. Wiping the sweat from her brow, and clicking her neck, Dr Maronne prepared herself for the inevitable firefight. Taking a deep breath she looked down the sight of her Las-Carbine and as the arm of a single blackjack rounded the corner, she opened fire. With the precision of a sharpshooter she connected with four bursts, the black metallic arm melting under sustained impact; sparks of electrical flame flittering about the appendage. Before the blackjack could turn and return fire, Maronne released a fusion grenade from her belt, clicked the activation pin twice and rolled it down the hall. As Keifar pulled the manual release on the hanger doors, klaxons sounding all around and amber indicator lights signalling its opening, Dr Maronne's grenade detonated. At first, the hanger was filled with a mute pop and the sound of air hastily sucking inward. Then the huge explosive force reverberated throughout. Maronne dived to the ground, avoiding the burst of flame that ripped through the door. "We need to move," she yelled, as a mixture of dry wall and dust covered her prone body.

"That is becoming a catch phrase," Keifar responded, helping her up and into the back of the skimmer. By this point Nishfar had finished his pre-flight checks and was preparing to take off. As Maronne and Keifar loaded on board he turned to face them with a smile on his face, but his expression soon darkened. "Where is Mahira???" he questioned, looking all about the passenger compartment.

Both Keifar and Maronne froze, their expressions filled with fear. "She was here, I just loaded her on board before opening the hanger," Keifar responded, knocking aside crates and looking frantically about the compartment. As if in slow motion, Nishfar peered out the drivers display and his heart sank. Instinctively he released the belt clasp, darted into the passenger compartment and out of the door. Mahira was in the hanger, grabbing 'Ikle Paulie', she must have dropped him. Keifar tried to stop his brother and go in his stead, but he was not fast enough. Nishfar moved across the hanger like a blur. As Maronne instinctively leapt out to cover Nishfar, Keifar likewise dived into the pilot seat and triggered the ignition. The Blackjacks, now reduced in number thanks to the grenade but still three strong, burst through the door. Two of them took aim towards Mahira and Nishfar, the other to Maronne. As one, they all opened fire. Nishfar leapt towards his daughter, eyes filled with intent. Mahira clutched 'Ikle Paulie' tightly, turning away from the fear inducing drones, her tearful eyes meeting her father's. Maronne was able to take cover behind one of the legs of the skimmer, their fire ricocheting off the metal.

The charging of a railgun reverberated throughout the hangar. Nishfar landed in front of his daughter and grabbed her tightly in his arms, sliding towards the edge of the wall beyond. The railgun shot penetrated the air. Nishfar's eyes widened. Keifar watched on from within the skimmer, powerless as his brother gasped for air when the railgun shot pierced his lower back and exited his stomach, narrowly missing Mahira.

Keifar cried out, his face grimacing, his world imploding with unforgiving ferocity. Maronne's pain wasn't nearly as intense yet it still fuelled her anger. She popped her head out from behind the leg and opened fire, switching to full auto. Nishfar looked into his daughter's eyes, drawing her attention away from his wound. She was crying, as was he, and he raised his hand to her face to wipe away her tears with his thumb. "Do not cry sweetheart," he whispered, his voice staggered as his breathing fought against the pain. "You're safe now. We...saved you."

"Daddy, you can't go, not to the stars, not yet," she wept, her voice broken by pain. Despite his attempts to ease her sorrow, he watched on as his daughter was consumed by the pain of losing her father. By this point the Blackjacks had advanced closer to the skimmer. Maronne was firing upon them, hate in her eyes. Her sustained fire melted and fractured pieces of the armour but it did not stop them. With very few options she reached down towards her belt, to retrieve a standard grenade. As she did so a shot caught her in the arm, she didn't react. With little thought for the blast range, she triggered the pin on the grenade and threw it to the feet of the Blackjacks. Seconds later an explosion reverberated outward, taking the first Blackjack with it and showering the room in shrapnel. Maronne took several hits to the face, body, and legs, her blood spraying everywhere, but her adrenaline kept her focused.

Keifar channelled his pain into rage. He felt every ounce of his body tense with anger, the very fabric of his being fuelled by an insatiable need for vengeance. Grabbing his own rifle he leapt out of the skimmer with little thought for his own safety. As the dust began to settle from the explosion his laser fire pierced through the smoke. He marched forward toward the last two remaining Blackjacks with furious indignation. The two drones couldn't react before he was upon them, Las-Carbine pressed firmly against the head of one. His finger pressed down upon the trigger with little remorse causing the drone's head to explode outward in a shower of blue flame and sparks. Its metallic carcass dropped to the floor. Before Keifar could react, the last remaining Blackjack struck him across the side of the face. Blood and teeth exploded from his mouth in a crimson haze. But Keifar, fuelled by the pain of his brother's mortal wound, showed little care. Immediately he returned the gesture with the butt of his rifle.

Using Keifar's bloodthirsty assault on the Blackjacks as cover, Dr Maronne moved over toward Nishfar and Mahira. She slid down behind the scholar with haste, slinging the Las-Carbine over her shoulder and lifting his shirt. The wound was horrific. Nishfar knew it and by the look in his daughter's eyes she knew too. He looked to Dr Maronne and grabbed her arm, his grip weakening as his life faded away. "You need to get her off the planet…promise me…promise me you and Keifar will get her to safety," he whispered, his words broken by staggered breaths. Blood started to run from his lips as his wound worsened. Maronne nodded, tears beginning to pool in her sorrowful eyes. She wiped the blood from his lips and applied pressure to his wound, knowing it was in vain. Nishfar turned back to Mahira and smiled. At this point he could no longer hold back his emotions, his strength fading. Both father and daughter began to cry. Nishfar cried in the knowledge that he would not get to see her grow up, whilst Mahira was overcome with the agonising sorrow of losing the father she loved so dearly. He reached out to hold her petite, tear covered face once more. The warmth of his hand brought a brief smile to her lips. "From the stars…we will always love you," he whispered, holding back his coughing to place a subtle kiss upon her forehead.

Keifar stood over the crumpled, sparking remnant of the final blackjack. His nose was broken, blood was dripping from his nostrils and mouth, and his eyes bloodshot. Instinctively he knew his brother was dead. Part of him didn't want to turn around, unable to face the stark and painful realisation that his brother was gone.

Dr Maronne placed her fingers over Nishfar's eyelids, closing them. "He's safe now Mahira," she continued, "he's gone to the stars. He's with Mummy now." Mahira was inconsolable, tears now streaming freely from her eyes, her grip on 'ikle paulie' tighter than it had ever been before.

The sound of metal upon metal reverberated down the hallway as backup drew ever closer. Maronne picked Mahira up in her arms and rushed her towards the skimmer, loading her and 'ikle paulie' into the back. She then moved toward Keifar and grabbed him by the arm. "Come on General!" she asked, her tone subtle and caring, her grip lighter than usual. "My brother?" Keifar asked, his eyes fixed upon the door with exasperation.

"He saved her, but he is gone," she responded, channelling her heart felt grief through her hand. Keifar's heart cracked under the weight of his brother's loss. He turned around slowly and as his eyes met Nishfar's lifeless body, he broke. Keifar raised his fist to his mouth, trying to block the exclamation of anguish as he bit down on his knuckles. He was a strong man, but the loss of his brother hit him harder than any physical wound he had every suffered. "We're taking him with us!" he exclaimed, marching towards the body,

"We don't have time!" Dr Maronne responded contritely.

"WE ARE NOT LEAVING HIM!" Keifar snapped back, his eyes filled with grim determination. Dr Maronne knew she couldn't contest him and instead turned to face the door, raising her Las-Carbine to cover him.

When Keifar reached his brothers body, his eyes were a torrent of tears, his face filled with unimaginable sorrow. He lowered himself to kneel beside his brother's body, cradling Nishfar's head in his arms and immediately lost control, burying his head in his brother's chest. "I'm sorry!" he cried out. "I'm sorry I couldn't save you…but I won't let you down again, I will get Mahira out, I will get her off this planet…and then, Stars help me, I will avenge you!"

"We have to go Keifar!" Maronne yelled. "There are more than we can handle!"

Lifting his brother in his arms, Keifar marched toward the skimmer, carefully lifting his body into the rear compartment. Upon seeing her father once more, Mahira turned away as she continued to weep. Keifar placed his brother down with care, laying a sheet of tarpaulin over him, and turned to his niece. With both their expressions filled with near overwhelming grief he placed his hand upon her and gently nuzzled her face to his chest. "You're safe with me!" he whispered. At that point Maronne leapt in through the hatch and struck the closing switch. Her eyes spoke a thousand words and Keifar leapt into the pilot seat, kicked the H.S.L.A. into gear and launched it out of the hanger door.

***

The skimmer sped low across the tree line, Keifar careful to avoid any collisions. His eyes were filled with tears and had been ever since they'd left the Arcology. He was still in shock and denial, in his mind he could hear Maronne spouting psychology 101 and the five stages of grief, but that didn't help matters. Keifar was immediately thrust into a bottomless pit of despair, unable to accept his brother was gone. His world swiftly felt overwhelming, the task of protecting his niece in the absence of his brother unfathomable.

"Initiate auto-pilot," Keifar commanded.

"Auto-pilot engaged," the artificial intelligence responded with a pleasance unsuited to the melancholic atmosphere inside the skimmer. Dr Maronne moved into the co-pilot seat and placed her hand upon Keifar's shoulder, bringing him a much needed warmth. He placed his free hand upon hers and feigned a smile, but it wasn't enough to hide his pain. "He can't be dead," he lamented, "I can't have failed him."

"It's OK, Keifar," Maronne responded. "You're in denial, but there is grace in denial, its humanities way of allowing you only as much as you can handle."

"I promised Dad I would always look out for Nishfar," he continued, "with the bullies, with mum, stars lament I even had to stick up for him against Layla at times."

"Nishfar wouldn't want you to be sad," Maronne continued, "I didn't know him long. But it was long enough to realise that he was a man of purpose, even if his purpose was knowledge. Now that Mahira is relying on you, you need to step up. The time for mourning will come."

131

"I will be stronger," Keifar responded, looking her in the eyes, his expression portraying his love for her, "for you, for Mahira, for Neesh."

"WARNING! WARNING! WARNING!" the artificial intelligence exclaimed, interrupting their conversation. "Imminent exterior collision. Alter Course! Alter Course! Alter Course!" The holo-display was also illuminated by equally abrupt warnings of collision.

Startled, Keifar jumped into action, taking hold of the control stick and disengaging autopilot. But as he looked out the front view port he could see no obstructions. Choosing to air on the side of caution he pulled the skimmer into a sharp, starboard turn. No sooner had he done so was he forced into another evasive manoeuvre as seemingly out of nowhere earth, rocks, trees and other foliage exploded upward from the forest below. It was an eruption Keifar barely avoided, the skimmer taking a few glancing hits and getting covered in a thin layer of dirt, but they were safe.

From amongst the rubble and debris a ship more than forty feet in diameter and near three times as tall, burst forth from the ground, hurtling skyward at astonishing speed. It bore no markings and was of no design Keifar had ever seen in his life. Antique rockets, a form of propulsion not used since the dawn of colonial space travel, propelled it toward atmosphere and beyond. "He can't have been right!" Keifar exclaimed with a mixture of disbelief and joy.

"What in the stars is that?" Dr Maronne exclaimed, her voice filled with shock and awe. Keifar pulled away from the launch in order to get a better view.

"It's a colonial age contingency failsafe," Keifar answered, "they were supposedly a myth. My brother was fascinated by them growing up, he always insisted they existed yet no one had ever seen one."

Keifar manually engaged hover, turning his full attention toward the ship as it disappeared into high atmosphere.

"Contingency failsafe?" Dr Maronne questioned, transfixed by what she was witnessing.

"My brother, and many other scholars, theorised that every planet designated for colonisation had them. Vessels prepared in case of a catastrophic planetary event," Keifar continued, "our

Grandfather supposedly remembered the day they were installed, even worked on them. But we all thought it was crazy. Everyone but Neesh of course."

"So somebody found it, and used it?" Dr Maronne interjected, displaying a clear understanding and yet her words were tinged with a hint of sorrow. "That would have been a way to get Mahira off world."

"Exactly," Keifar continued with new found excitement, "someone has obviously worked out how to activate them."

"Them?" Dr Maronne questioned with an equally inquisitive gesture. "You think there are more?"

"My brother thought there were multiple. If there is one then I have faith Neesh was right about the others," Keifar answered, his expression of disbelief never fading.

Three minutes passed before the contingency shuttle disappeared out of view. Keifar took control of the skimmer again and lowered its altitude beneath the tree line. "Open communication. Channel: Zero, Eight, Eight, Point Nine, Six, Three, Identification: General Keifar Montiz, Authorisation Code: Whisky, Charlie, Alpha, Foxtrot, Eight, Eight, Zero," he spoke, commanding the artificial intelligence into action,

"Confirm. Channel open," the AI responded after a brief intermission. "General? Is that you?" a familiar voice spoke through the radio, Keifar smiled. "Romero!!!" he acknowledged. "Damn good to hear your voice."

"The feeling is mutual General. Do you have the cargo?" Romero continued. It dulled Keifar's moment of joy.

"Confirmed….but… Nishfar didn't make it," Keifar responded, a lump in his throat. Romero fell silent. Keifar knew the pilot would feel responsible, but it wasn't his fault. "I'm…sorry General," Romero eventually replied.

"It isn't your fault, Romero, you have no need to apologise. Getting shot out the sky is not something any pilot can predict, nor necessarily avoid," Keifar responded, bottling up the torrent of emotions that begged to be free.

"I still feel responsible," Romero continued.

"Well don't. That's an order!" Keifar replied, his voice containing a faint mirth.

"I suppose you want to land," Romero said, returning to formal matters. "Hanger one is free."

"This facility only has one hanger?" Keifar countered,

"Exactly. After the Arcology, it's free," Romero caustically responded.

Keifar instantly felt apologetic. He realised Romero's beloved shuttle had obviously not survived its hit at the Arcology. With that in mind, Keifar inquisitively wondered how Romero had returned to base with such haste. That was a question for a later date.

"Confirm. Approaching Hanger One. Eta two minutes," Keifar commanded, his fingers darting frantically across the H.S.L.A. control panel.

***

As they stepped off the shuttle Mahira wouldn't let go of Keifar, her grip tighter than any hug she had ever given him before. He embraced it, not wanting to forsake her at this time when they both grieved for the loss of his brother. Neither he nor Dr Maronne could comprehend what the young girl was going through. This war had taken from her both parents, worse still she had witnessed the death of her father first hand. A memory that could never be undone.

Laying a subtle kiss upon her head, Keifar held her close. A medical crew was on standby as soon as the skimmer had touched down, accompanying Romero to greet the arrivals. By this point Maronne was beginning to show signs of exhaustion and fatigue, more so than Keifar. This coupled with the wounds she had sustained in the line of fire, and the shrapnel cuts to her face, caused her to collapse welcomingly onto the awaiting stretcher.

"I need stitches on my forehead, left cheek and lower left jaw as well as an x-ray of my left Humerus, Scapula and Clavicle," she ordered, her words staggered and filled with fatigue. "Also. Fluids. Lots of fluids. I'm so thirsty. And I have a slight back ache... We might want to do a scan for Kidney lacerations as well."

"Good job you're with the doctor," Keifar smiled, gripping her shoulder affectionately. "I appreciate everything you did back there... Thank you."

Maronne placed her own hand upon his with fondness and nodded, "You don't need to thank me. Whether you like it or not, you're family now."

Her words brought a slight smile to Mahira, the pair of them exchanging an affectionate look. "I'll check in on you later." Keifar responded,

"Hopefully I won't need surgery," Maronne lamented with a sarcastic yet equally worried smile, "because I am the best surgeon here...the only surgeon here."

"His body is in the passenger compartment," Keifar sorrowfully disclosed, turning to face a corpsman. "Have the medical team prep him for burial."

"Very well General," the corpsman responded, stepping onboard the shuttle and signalling for an assistant to join him. Keifar wanted to stay and help, yet at the same time he didn't want Mahira to have to see her father's body again. "We'll have the service later today," Keifar announced, raising his voice to attract the attention of everyone in the hanger. "Let it be known that Nishfar Montiz was a hero. A man who risked everything to save his own. He is the reason our free army still stands strong."

"AYE!" a cacophony of voices yelled in response. "May the Stars protect him!"

The passion of the crowd, and the respect in their response, brought a smile to both he and Mahira. It was a smile they very much needed.

Mahira was overwhelmed. Her emotions fuelled a childlike shyness as she buried her head into Keifar's chest. It was enough to bring a further tear to his eye. Despite all his strength, Keifar Montiz finally showed a sincere humanity. Wishing not to display his sorrow for long, Keifar nodded to his men and women then turned toward the exit. Falling into step beside him, Romero patted him on the back and gave him a courteous nod. "Permission to speak freely?" he asked,

"Permission granted," Keifar responded, holding Mahira ever closer.

"You need to take time to grieve general. You're no use to this army when plagued by your brother's passing!" Romero said, as the pair of them entered the corridor adjoining the hanger. "By all means use his death to fuel your resolve, but take the time to make sure it doesn't cloud your judgement. I'm speaking as a friend."

Keifar looked at Romero directly, his eyes giving little of his feelings away. For those briefest of seconds, Romero tensed. "Romero!" Keifar replied, his tone lowered, "I respect your opinion. But right now my priority is not this army, nor the freedom of Hakon IV. It's my niece, and to my brother's dying wish for her to get off this world and away from this war!"

Romero paused, unsure if he had just been chastised or not. Choosing to air on the side of caution, he responded plainly.

"Then right now, the army's priority is Mahira!" he said with a smile, warmly punching Keifar on the upper arm. "Let's get her off this planet, son!"

"Thank you," Keifar replied with a heartfelt smile. "And, for the umpteenth time, I'm the same age as you. Please don't call me son."

"OK…son," Romero jested, his smirk portraying his continued sense of humour.

As Keifar exited without him, and the medical staff wheeled Dr Maronne off for some much needed attention, Romero's face went as white as a full moon. He turned to one of the operations staff that had remained with him and sighed. "Our priority has to be the girl now," he said, his voice tinged with melancholy. "For the general."

"You didn't tell him!" the operations corporal replied with an authority above her station. Romero paused, his skin returning to its normal complexion,

"I didn't tell him because right now his responsibility is to his family!" he said, his voice replete with barely suppressed anger. "For stars' sake he just lost his brother, his future wife is wounded, and he's just become the soul guardian of his niece. He doesn't need me, need any of us, to darken his mood any further with needless politics."

"But surely he should know that the government of Hakon IV has fallen," the Corporal replied, braving the possibility of Romero's rage.

"Keifar saw it coming. He knew the Office of Planetary Affairs would out grow its mandate," Romero replied with now unsuppressed rage, "considering the events of the Soleri Arcology, I doubt he hasn't already considered the possibility of them committing a coo. So I repeat, he doesn't need to know the government has fallen because he no doubt already assumes as much."

The operations corporal bowed her head in deference, "Sorry sir, I was out of line."

"No lass, don't apologise," Romero continued with a smile, calming as he placed a hand upon the young women's shoulder. "You were right to question me, keep me honest, but in this case we need to follow my advice and that's an order."

Romero wasn't a man to use his rank often, in truth he held a great deal of distaste for the hierarchy of authority. But even he knew that now, without Dr Maronne or the General in a fit state to command, he was the next best thing. He accepted the burden without second thought.

Chapter Twelve

Mahira fell asleep on the cold, hard mattress at the base of Keifar's bunk. The young girl was fatigued and emotionally broken, falling asleep as soon as her head hit the crudely constructed pillow. Keifar found himself just staring at her as she slept, hypnotised by the serenity. For the briefest of moments he felt at peace, but it wouldn't last. A hard knock sounded at his door. With haste he leapt to his feet, eager to catch the door before a further knock could awaken his niece. Practically putting his palm through the door's command console, he slammed the open switch. As the door slid to the side, he placed a finger to his lips in a gesture for silence. The female corporal, petite and clearly fresh out of training, froze. "Sorry sir!" she exclaimed in a whisper. "I didn't mean to disturb you."

Keifar slid into the hallway as if across ice and closed the door behind him.

"Don't worry, Corporal," he whispered as the door slid shut, his voice returning to normal. "I just didn't want to wake the girl."

"Yes sir," she replied with a respectful nod. "Flight Captain Romero sent me to get you. Cass has been asking to see you, she says it is urgent."

"I suppose I had to engage her in conversation sooner or later," Keifar answered despondently. "She at least needs to know that Nishfar is dead."

***

Keifar nodded to the guard stationed at the entrance of the brig. It was makeshift, a ramshackle construction of hastily welded bars and metal plates. The base didn't have designated holding facilities so they had repurposed an old armament storage room, turning it into a brig. In the right cell, affectionately known as the drunk tank, a couple of rookies sat looking sorry for themselves. By the bruises and cuts it appeared to be another night of drunken debauchery gone awry. In the left cell, doing ab crunches as regimentally as she had been every day, Cass stared blankly into space. "Open up Cell One!" Keifar commanded to the guard, gesturing toward the door with his hand. "Very well sir. Are you armed?" the guard responded, offering out his own sidearm,

"My legs are titanium and I have a reinforced spine," Keifar joked, "if she can take me down without a weapon, she deserves freedom. Stand down soldier!"

"Very well, General," the guard responded, replacing his sidearm and entering the code for the cell door. The familial whoosh of the door broke Cass free from her exercise induced day dream, forcing her attention toward Keifar.

"I did not think you would come," she exclaimed, standing to her feet and dusting herself off, "I asked for Nishfar to come see me also, but he hasn't been by."

"He would find that quite hard," Keifar replied, his voice tinged with vehement distaste he could do little to hide,

"He's left?" Cass questioned. "Did he return to Mahira?"

"You could say he left," Keifar continued, rolling up his sleeves. "Cass...he's dead."

Despite a failed attempt to disguise her body language Cass' face went as white as ivory, her expression darkening with sadness. "Dead? Did I?" she questioned expectantly. Keifar found himself momentarily considering a mean streak and, despite the cynicism involved, leading her to believe she had in the hope she would feel the pain as he had. But those thoughts were silenced by his sense of honour.

"No," he responded, plainly, "he was killed by a Blackjack, back at the Arcology, killed protecting the one thing that mattered the most to him."

"Mahira is still alive?" Cass questioned. "He wanted to do everything to get her away from this war, I would have done anything to help him."

"Including kill me?" Keifar snapped, his tone filled with intense disdain. "How would killing me have helped him save Mahira?"

"Because your death could have ended the war!" she replied, her tone showing blind faith with each word.

Keifar stepped towards her, diverting his eyes away for fear inciting his boiling rage. "You truly believe that don't you?" he questioned, biting his lip to avoid inflaming the situation further. "How far you have fallen Cass?"

A cold silence filled the holding cell as the pair paced around each other, neither meeting the eyes of the other. It was akin to a duel, all the nuances of a sword fight yet without the swords.

"So whilst I stand here you're planning to kill me, is that right?" Keifar asked, breaking the silence.

"What kind of soldier would I be if that were not the case?" she responded, her arms noticeably tensing, her fists tightly clenched.

"An honourable one," Keifar continued, tensing his own muscles in preparation of her perceived, imminent assault. The attack never came.

"I didn't call you here to make another attempt on your life," Cass finally piped up, "I called you here to let you know something, to pass you much needed intel."

"How can I trust you?" Keifar questioned, considering her previous inclination. "You tried to kill my brother, you tried to kill me!"

"Because you can't afford to not trust me. You said yourself, war changes people. It changed me," Cass continued, relaxing noticeably, her head dropping. "I was following orders but now I have no government to follow, no constitution to protect. Everything I knew about our world, everything I agreed to fight for, everything I believed in, all of it up in smoke. You, Keifar Montiz, are my only chance at redemption."

"What is the intel?" Keifar asked, snapping straight to the point, his expression betraying no love lost. "I'll decide whether we can use you once you've told me."

"Do you promise my freedom?" Cass questioned expectantly.

"Not until your information is proven. Ergo I guess you'll be the one taking the gamble on my honesty," Keifar answered, a snide smile crossing his lips. "What will it be Cass?"

"The Office of Planetary Affairs has a contingency in place. I was privy to that contingency," she began, sitting on the metallic slab that formed a rudimentary bed. "A contingency to take control of all planetary assets… I guess you could say…"

"A military coup masquerading as a way to protect the people!" Romero interjected as the cell door slid open. "Keifar I didn't mean for you to hear like this, but the government has fallen. The O.P.A. committed a coup, Hakon IV is under martial law now. The Blackjacks, they're the enforcers, they're everywhere."

"Do we have enemy numbers?" Keifar asked, turning to face Romero.

"Well it turns out that the O.P.A. had more assets in play than previously thought. Not including Cass, there are at least four spooks in our AO," Romero continued, glancing toward Cass. "These spooks in turn feed forward intel to the Blackjacks. The drones, we presume, then execute the various attacks."

"Everything that has happened, this war, the collateral damage, the press coverage, all of it is part of a bigger plan by the O.P.A." Cass interjected, her tone commanding, her body language displaying a strength of character not seen since the Marine Core. "They are the enemy here, they used me, I realise that now."

Keifar looked at her inquisitively, unsure how to take her new found realisation. The betrayal she had committed tore a hole through his trust and friendship so wide it could swallow the suns. He doubted it would ever truly be repaired. Now, with the death of his brother and the adoption of Mahira, he had a lot to deal with and trusting Cass was the least of his worries.

"Madam President was worried about the failing economy, but so confident in repairing it that she made a deal with the devil, she has paid the price for that hubris," Cass continued, maintaining the attention of both of them. "There is also a chance she has paid the ultimate price and is now six feet under, we will probably never know. When I joined the Marines I swore allegiance to the planet, to the constitution of the colony, not a person. I said the exact same thing to Nishfar before I betrayed you both. That still stands true and the O.P.A aren't what is best for the planet. Therefore I want to help you take it back."

"I'll never forgive you," Keifar sternly replied, "and I doubt I will ever be able to trust you again, but begrudgingly I have to acknowledge you're a damn good fighter and an even better doctor. The F.H.A. needs people like you."

"I guess that's welcome aboard," Romero piped up, his tone less than welcoming as his eyes betrayed his antipathy toward the situation, "be warned there are more than a handful of people here who'd rather see you dead."

"I work better alone," Cass replied, a sly smirk crossing her lips, "and, I guess, never with you Keifar."

"I'm staying away from you, and you away from me!" Keifar commanded, his voice teeming with animosity, "you want to do something for the better of the F.H.A. then find those other spooks in this AO and deal with them."

"Right away…General," she replied with a genuine salute, "for what it's worth, I am sorry."

"I don't care for apologies," Keifar retorted, turning to walk away, "actions speak louder than words."

Keifar was intent on returning to Mahira when Romero fell into step beside him. "Permission to speak," he requested, his tone portraying a degree of levity following the previous conversation.

"Stop asking for permission fly boy!" Keifar responded in jest.

"Very well son," Romero said, giving rise to a sarcastic grin, "I took the liberty of making some enquiries based on our current objective."

"I told you, Romero, my priority is Mahira right now," Keifar interjected, wishing not to hear of objectives and strategies in his current mind set. He was still struggling with his brother's passing and now he had found out that the world he fought so hard for was crumbling. Further still he was forced to put into play an asset that had betrayed him once before, a person whom had once been family. At this time he wasn't strong enough to be the General the F.H.A wanted, let alone needed. It was his job nonetheless.

"And I told you that Mahira was our priority too, did I not?" Romero retorted with continued levity. "As I was saying, I took the liberty of making some enquiries based on our current objective." Keifar's expression brightened slightly as he now took interest in what the pilot had to say. It was a welcome distraction from the pain he had yet to truly confront.

"When your skimmer was returning you nearly collided with a colonial age shuttle, right?" Romero asked. "I found this out based on the skimmers telemetry and data-bank readings…that and Dr Maronne would not stop mentioning it."

"That's my girl, we did indeed. One of the contingency shuttles," Keifar said with an inquisitive tone of voice, "I recognised it as soon as I saw it, Neesh was obsessed with them but everyone thought them to be a conspiracy."

Romero nodded, "Hakon IV supposedly has eight of these vessels, the one that launched earlier was Contingency Two from our estimates," he continued as the pair of them walked through a large set of double doors. "Refugees from the Soleri Arcology, most of them in some way related to the civil service, managed to board and launch it," Romero proceeded, himself more animated than before, "now Contingency Three and Contingency Four are both presumed destroyed however our scouts have reported a large contingent of refugees amassing in an area due south of here. In a previously unidentified bunker."

"You think one of the vessels is stored there?" Keifar interjected, his expression brightening further with the spark of hope, his eyes widening.

"I don't think, I know!" Romero beamed. "With the government lock down of space flight and the O.P.A's subsequent coup, the only way off world has been via these virtually indestructible beasts, all other vessels are shot out the sky by the super cruisers. So I had our scouts investigate the place and they discovered both Contingency Three and Contingency Four."

"I need to get Mahira on one of those vessels," Keifar exclaimed, gripping Romero by both shoulders in jubilation. "That's her ticket away from this war!"

"I knew you'd say as much. I've already prepped the skimmer and a small team to escort you. I'll fly," Romero nodded.

"As much as I appreciate the gesture Romero, and truly I do, I need someone I can trust here to lead this resistance whilst I'm gone," Keifar continued, looking him directly in the eyes with piercing intent.

"She knew you'd say that," Romero replied, his smug expression difficult to hide. "Dr Maronne has volunteered to stay behind. As Colonel she is more than qualified to lead the resistance in your absence."

"That woman never ceases to amaze me," Keifar replied with a contented laugh, in that moment he could have kissed her had she been present. "She is an astounding woman, her willingness to stay behind is a testament to that. Although she must know this means she may never see me again." With that realisation a tear began to form in Keifar's eye, the war taking its toll on his already challenged emotions.

"Wheels up in an hour," Romero continued, slapping Keifar on the back. "We need to move hastily before the refugees launch both…"

"Make it two. There is something I have to do first," Keifar interrupted. "I need to bury my brother."

***

Keifar looked out through the vast forest with a desolate stare. His eyes teeming with regret. The toll of a thousand emotional wounds in his battle warn visage. His skin was haggard, his eyes darkened by little sleep, and his jaw quivered with fatigue. Despite all this he had taken the time to change into his dress uniform, proudly brandishing the colours of the Hakon IV Marine Core. The uniform had a form fitting, long-sleeved, crimson red coat with a black standing collar and white web belt. His former rank, gunnery sergeant, as a gold waist-plate. A peaked cap with attached rank insignia, plain white shirt, crimson red trousers, white gloves, and black dress shoes completed the ensemble. On the left of his chest he proudly wore his full-size service medals and on his right several of his combat ribbons, a mixture of exemplary marksmanship, survival and leadership under fire. Despite Keifar's opposition to the authorities, he still felt proud of the Core and all it had originally stood for. He dreamt of a day when it would once again fight for a just cause.

Mahira stood next to him, 'Ikle Paulie' clenched tightly to her chest, her head buried in the teddy's warm fur. Behind the pair of them, forty men and women of the Free Hakon Army stood to attention, the coffin containing Nishfar to their left ready to be carried. Dr Maronne, herself in similar dress uniform,

144

yelled out commands and with synchrony the men and women turned to face the coffin. Keifar placed a caring hand on Mahira's shoulder and the pair exchanged a warm smile, an expression that did little to shield the near overwhelming pain both of them felt. Romero marched up toward Keifar, bowed his head with respect and then crouched in front of Mahira in order to offer the same respects. "We're ready," he whispered, rising once more to his feet and gesturing toward the front of the group with his arm.

"You stay close to us Mahira," Keifar said affectionately, grasping her shoulder lightly. "Let's give Daddy the send-off to the Stars he deserves."

Keifar walked to the front of the group and up to his brother's casket. Turning to face his men and women, he smiled. Despite the sorrow of the day his expression brightened with great respect. That these men and women had taken time out of their already strained schedules to pay tribute to his brother was as poignant as it was appreciated. "Men, Women, and Children," he called out, his voice booming. "We gather here today to pay respects to a hero, a man who sacrificed everything for the safety of his own, who risked, and ultimately paid with, his life. He was a man who saw the truth in everything, wanting nothing more than to help everyone he encountered. Nishfar Montiz, my brother, Mahira's father, will live on in our memory not as someone we lost but as someone we should aspire to be. Our strength, our direction, our will to succeed, all of these things we must take from the memory of Nishfar Montiz. We fight with renewed strength because of him!"

"Aye sir!" The crowd yelled, every one of them stamping their right leg in unison as a sign of respect.

"I require five volunteers to assist me in shouldering his casket," Keifar continued, a tear swelling in his eye. "May we send him to the stars."

The group marched forward, casket borne upon their shoulders. Keifar led them from the front, carrying the weight with pride. Behind them the remaining thirty five men and women walked in formation, Las-Carbines pressed against their shoulders. To the rear a lone soldier played a bugle, its tune breaking the silence with a forlorn melody. It was a beautiful sight, one Nishfar would have been honoured by. That thought brought the emotion raging forth from within Keifar's heart, a torrent of uncontrollable tears streaming down his face. But he cared little for appearances. Now was the time to mourn. Mahira, walking alongside Dr Maronne, was near inconsolable, clenching 'Ikle Paulie' tighter and tighter with every footfall. The little girl could barely see through her tears as she sobbed and Dr Maronne soon found herself sobbing alongside, despite her attempts to remain strong.

It was an honourable march toward the burial site, a clearing approximately fifty feet in diameter that already housed several graves of the fallen. Many of the Free Hakon Army tended to the burial site in their free time, others choosing to guard it when off duty. The memories of those whom had passed on to the stars was something every soldier took pride in regardless of race, religion or creed. The clearing reflected that pride. At the centre surrounded by a newly established arrangement of four stone slabs lay a freshly dug grave marked by a new headstone. Carved of the purest obsidian it was engraved with Nishfar's name, the years of his life and finally the respectful speech just given. Upon seeing it Keifar could only smile, his tears subsiding for the briefest of moments. The casket bearers marched up to the grave and slowly lowered the casket onto the hemp rope, ready to lower it down. As Keifar took a step back, Dr Maronne and Mahira joined him and he warmly took them in his arms. Caring little for the ramifications of their relationship becoming public knowledge, Maronne laid a subtle kiss upon his cheek that instantly soothed his pain and filled his heart with warmth. Taking a deep breath, he turned to face his men and women once more.

"Today we mourn!" he announced, choosing not to wipe the sign of tears from his cheeks. "We mourn not just the passing of my brother, but also the morals he stood for. As I said before, our renewed strength, our direction, our will, all of these things we must take from his memory." Mahira tugged lightly on Keifar's ceremonial coat and he looked down towards her with a smile.

"Daddy loved all of us, he hated fighting," she whispered. "Tell them he hated fighting!"

Keifar paused, laying a calm hand upon his niece's shoulder and nodding. "Nishfar despised conflict. He hated fighting," Keifar commanded, his voice bellowing out across the amassed crowd. "Our purpose, our fight, is to end this conflict. We must all strive to see an end to the fighting!"

Everyone erupted with cheer, fists raised into the air with a mixture of smiles and nods. The very concept of an end to the fighting brought hope to everyone and instilled in them a sense that their fight would be the last fight Hakon IV would need suffer. Nishfar's memory, everything he stood for, would be the catalyst for change the planet needed. But for Keifar there was a further purpose to his words and to the immortalisation of his brother, he needed the men and women to have the faith and resolve to continue the fight in his absence. "Please join me in a minute's silence," he continued, ending the rapturous exaltation of the crowd. "Whether you knew him or not, let us remember Nishfar Montiz."

The world around them fell all but silent, the light breeze whistling through the plush green trees that surrounded the clearing and the long grass at its furthest edges. In the distance the sound of conflict reminded all that a war still raged, but here, in the absence of the fighting, there was peace. For a brief time, those gathered need not know only war. Despite the forlorn nature of the gathering, Keifar's zealous words and the following silence brought a renewed faith to all who had attended. Regardless of the inconsolable pain eating away at his heart, the expressions of Keifar's men and women drew him back from the all-consuming black hole of grief. Their commitment, their dedication, it made everything worth it.

Keifar looked down at Mahira, who grabbed his leg tightly. She looked up to him and for the first time since her dad had died, she smiled. It was in that moment Keifar's mind was set and he knew he had to leave; his army would be fine without him. "Thank you," he commanded, ending the minute's silence, "you have made this day weigh less upon my soul and those of my family. Let us lower him into the ground, so he may return to the stars!"

With those words the bearers took a hold of the hemp rope and lowered the casket slowly into the grave. The lone bugle once again played its morose tune, the anthem of passing all soldiers dreaded yet wholeheartedly respected. Once lowered, Keifar and Mahira dropped flowers on to the casket before shovelling the first dirt together. Shortly after Dr Maronne and

Romero joined, followed by the bearers. As the mud obscured the casket, Keifar and Mahira looked to the sky above and the stars beyond. Holding his hat to his heart, the General placed a loving arm around his niece's shoulders and took a knee. "Goodbye my brother," he whispered to the stars.

***

An hour passed. The group of men and women had dispersed, Romero leading them back to base with haste. Keifar, Dr Maronne and Mahira remained facing the freshly turned earth upon Nishfar's grave. Above them the skies darkened, obscuring the battlecruisers that had amassed in high atmosphere. Rain began to pour. Under the torrential cascade of water the three of them remained motionless.

"You didn't tell them," Dr Maronne asserted, affectionately placing a hand to Keifar's cheek. "You should have told them."

"At my brother's funeral?" Keifar exclaimed.

"I'm not saying a funeral is the best place. But it was the most opportune time, with the most eyes and ears present. You won't get another chance before you head out," she responded, her eyes illustrating her genuine concern for him, "also, your brother's death, whether we like it or not, is a catalyst that will help them fight harder. You could have used that renewed vigour to announce your departure, I think they accept its inevitability they just need to hear it."

"I wanted to be sure you were OK with this," he replied, affectionately placing his own hand against her cheek. "We may never see each other again. Are you sure you are OK with that? Because I certainly don't know if I am."

As Keifar spoke, Mahira gripped his leg tighter and her display of affection strengthened his resolve.

"You have to," Dr Maronne continued, "she is the most important thing right now, for Nishfar."

"I will miss you!" he said, tears mixing with the rain. Dr Maronne could not hold back her own emotions and she too began to cry. The pair embraced each other's lips, an act both of them hoped would not be their last.

Chapter Thirteen

Keifar packed the last of his rations into the bulking rucksack upon his bunk. He had no idea what provisions would be available aboard the contingency shuttle and he didn't want Mahira to go hungry. She stood in the doorway behind him, 'Ikle Paulie' clenched tightly in her arms, a subdued smile across her expression. Upon her back she carried a small, pink, backpack with a floral pattern, a replacement for Mega-Cat whom she lost in the Arcology. It was full to breaking point with the zip barely able to contain the contents. Despite its crammed nature and associated weight, Mahira appeared unfazed. Instead she was more interested in 'Ikle Paulie's' comfort. Stroking him on the head, she gathered a little cloth handkerchief from her pocket and neatly wrapped him in it, a makeshift blanket to assure he was snug and warm. Laying a subtle kiss upon his forehead, she smiled. "I'll keep you safe," she whispered, "just like everyone is keeping me safe." Her words brought a smile to Keifar's lips. The comfort was short lived.

Klaxons began to blare all around them, the red hue of battle stations illuminating the room in which they stood. Mahira frantically looked around with fear and bewilderment. Keifar's head dropped. "Why now?" he whispered bitterly.

The stentorian rumble of war began. "Ladies and Gentleman," Dr Maronne's voice boomed out across the facility tannoy, distracting from the thunderous roar of aerial bombardment, "this is not a drill! We are under attack, repeat we are under attack. All soldiers report to your battle stations, all major access points on lock down. We face both ground and aerial threats. Steel yourselves, you have all prepared for this day. May the stars be with us!"

Keifar darted across his quarters and slammed his hand against the comm panel. "Colonel I'm inbound, prepare situation report, over," he commanded with authority. As he released the button a flustered yet flight prepared Romero came sprinting down the corridor, skidding to a halt at the door.

"Combined government and insurgent forces," the ace pilot said, catching his breath. "The Blackjacks are in play, receiving aerial support from the Atmospheric Defence Force. This, this is a big play."

Keifar's heart sank, and his expression fell with it as Romero's did the same. Despite their best efforts Mahira could read them both like a book and tears began to well in her eyes. "Seems the OPA is making its final play of the game," Keifar continued, putting sarcastic emphasis on the word 'game'. "It seems all branches of the planetary military are onside, the supposed insurgency too. We are all that stands between them and domination."

"If the A.D.F. is in play then that skimmer is going to struggle!" Romero conceded, his shoulders dropping with dejection. "I'm good but High Speed Low Altitude is no good in a straight fly-off against the air force's Variable Altitude T400 Raiders. I should know, I used to fly them."

"Then we don't make it a straight race!" Keifar responded defiantly. "Take Mahira and my bag, get to the shuttle and prep it for flight. I have one more defensive play call up my sleeve."

"That's the Keifar I remember!" Romero smiled emphatically, clapping Keifar across the shoulders and then grabbing his bag. Keifar dropped to his knee and looked Mahira square in the eyes, laying a gentle kiss upon her forehead as he did so. "I promise, come what may, I will see you at that shuttle!" Keifar exclaimed, "Come whatever may."

"I believe you," Mahira smiled. His strength of purpose clearly rubbed off on her.

***

"Activate the anti-air defences!" Keifar yelled out, rushing through the command room door as he hastily donned his combat armour.

"General. But!" Dr Maronne exclaimed.

"No buts, I'm here to make sure Mahira and I get away safely," he responded, his eyes burning with determination. "One last play!"

"Stars be damned, is there no way I can persuade you otherwise?" Dr Maronne questioned, her eyes subtly pleading with him to reconsider his position. She knew it was in vain, her eyes said it all, but she had to try because her conscience demanded it.

"Romero is prepping flight and Mahira is with him," Keifar continued, "I plan to get the ball rolling and then join on them on evac. Romero said that speeder won't out run the A.D.F. Raiders, I'm planning to make it so it won't have to!" Keifar was about to start coordinating some of the immediate command staff when the doors to the command room burst open once more.

"Who now?" Dr Maronne sighed, resigned to the fact the man she loved was going nowhere and so others would rally to him. Flanked by Havoc, sporting a new dark crimson paint scheme, and a team of volunteers, the Corporal marched with renewed purpose.

"Sir, Romero said you're about to do something crazy," the Corporal announced, his expression burning with respect. "We're here to make sure you don't die doing it!"

"And we can't have you break a promise to that little girl now can we sir!" Havoc followed up, his metallic face feigning a frown.

"We're going topside with Ground to Air pods, we're going to provide a distraction for Romero," Keifar smiled, immediately gesturing to the holographic display before him. "It's not going to be pretty, I can't promise any of you will make it back in one piece and I won't order you to go."

"We're volunteering sir," the Corporal continued. "You're stuck with us!"

"Thank you, everyone," Keifar responded sincerely, shaking the Corporal's hand as he did so. Turning back to the holographic map, he folded his arms and quietly observed the real-time updates as they came through. After a brief period of calm, he gesticulated toward the holographic display then clenched his fist before pulling it back towards himself. The display reacted accordingly, focusing on the exterior clearing and then zooming in as Keifar pulled his fist back. "When the skies are clear, Romero is going to launch. He'll sink low under the tree line, to the side of here, and pick me up," he continued with a nod, pointing to the corresponding areas of the holographic map. "I

151

just need that window of opportunity, with it I am going to get Mahira to one of those contingency shuttles before they leave."

"Don't you fucking die, you promise me!" Dr Maronne commanded, grabbing Keifar by the scruff of his armour and looking directly into his eyes. Her stern words drew further silence from the command room, no one had ever spoken to the General like that before. "Her safety is paramount, I made a promise I'd get back to her and I don't intend on breaking it," he responded, his passion clear for all to hear.

"I love you," Dr Maronne replied without a thought or care for those who'd hear her. Before she could react to her indiscretion, Keifar drew her close and kissed her with a passion he never knew he had.

They shared their embrace for no more than a minute although, to the both of them, it felt like an eternity. Finally releasing her from his lips Keifar turned back to the screen, his arm still wrapped around her shoulders. With a content smile he motioned toward one of the communication officers, "Open all frequencies," he commanded. "Men and women of the Free Hakon Army, this is your general speaking. It is with the upmost sincerity that I hereby promote Colonel Maronne to the rank of Brigadier General, and pass command to her," Keifar announced with authority. "I have instructed her on all our plans moving forward and her first mission in command is to initiate protocol 'Three Sixteen,' may the stars be with us all."

Dr Maronne looked at him with surprise, "Three Sixteen?" she questioned.

"This base is a liability now, you won't hold the full force of the military off on your own. This way you can leave, regroup and live to fight another day," he responded passionately. "Plus they'll never see it coming, they never do!" With one last embrace the pair parted ways, their eyes fixed on each other until Keifar had left the room.

As he stepped out of view Dr Maronne straightened herself out, wiped away the tears welling in her eyes and clicked her neck from right to left. "Initiate base wide timer, 'Three Sixteen' is a go," she commanded with a smile upon her lips. "Let's show them what we are made of!"

***

"Romero?" Keifar yelled across the comm as his unit moved at pace through the facility. The world around them shook under sustained bombardment, dust and rubble falling with every strike.

Despite the hostile environment the group maintained focus. "This is Romero, over," the hot-shot pilot responded.

"I'm sending you co-ordinates, when I give the command I need you to launch and collect me from that point," Keifar commanded, never missing a step, "my play is live, repeat my play is live."

"Sir!" Havoc shouted, moving up alongside the general as they ran. "My sensors are detecting a breach at our surface exit point, two five man squads, no Blackjacks."

"You hear that team?" Keifar smirked. "We've got ourselves a welcome committee. Let us thank them personally."

Everyone simultaneously double checked their rifles and loaded their clips, the hiss of coolant reset reverberating all around, the sounds of conflict barely muting the synchronised metallic snap of every gun. "Havoc once we're top side I need you to go aerial," Keifar instructed, tapping the former journalist drone on the shoulder. "I know it's a risk, but I need eyes in the sky."

"I live for risk, General," Havoc responded with jest, "I used to be a combat journalist after all, they be *crazy*." The exit hallway was dark, with what little sun available beaming through the breached iron doors and illuminating its dusty interior. The Corporal took point, using a crudely crafted mirror on a stick to peer around the corner.

"Standard formation," he whispered, "five men either side attempting to use the shadows as cover. They're armed with Las-Carbines, no rifles, likely grenades. I can't get a visual on those at the back so they may have heavy support."

"Let's say hello," Keifar gestured before raising his rifle to a firing position. "Corporal, on you."

Waiting for the cover provided by another bombardment, the Corporal prepared two G45 flash-bang grenades. Unlike the more commonly used G25, the G45 provided both a brighter flash and louder 'bang' as well as a secondary dimmer flash, but due to a high mortality rate they saw little use across the colonies.

As a result the bunker was filled with crates full of them, crates the F.H.A. happily requisitioned.

With precision timing the battlecruisers, high above, reigned further heavy ordinance down upon the facility. The ground all around the unit shook with the ferocity of an earthquake but no one batted an eyelid, especially the Corporal. "Flash out," he whispered as he rolled the two G45s into the room. The grenades detonated in a bright flash shortly followed by the second. The unit, fronted by the Corporal and Havoc, burst around the corner and picked their targets with practiced ease. A hail of laser fire erupted all around, persisting for no more than a few seconds.

"Clear!" the Corporal announced, followed by a cacophony of responses from the other volunteers. Confident it was safe Keifar rounded the corner, his rifle still raised. Strewn either side of the exit ramp were the lifeless, smoking bodies of multiple Hakon IV marines. It was a sobering sight, seeing those he had such respect for dead at the hands of his own men. Keifar did his upmost to hold back the sorrow. *War changes people,* he thought to himself as he knelt down and lowered the eyelids of one of the deceased.

"Soldiers, brothers, sisters. When we step outside this hatch it will be hell," Keifar commanded pointing towards the sky outside, "those with Ground to Air pods I need you to get set-up as quickly as you can, do not wait for my command to open fire. Havoc head airborne and broadcast a broad frequency video link to update us with everything you see. Everyone else cover fire. Questions?"

"One," Havoc responded. "Will I get a medal?" The drone's words brought laughter to the group and a smile to Keifar's lips.

"Get me out of here and Maronne will give you all medals!" Keifar continued with a smirk, before returning to the business at hand. "Corporal when we have the window and I command Romero to launch I trust you can get me to the tree line?"

"Aye sir," the Corporal responded, "I will be covering your ass long before that General."

"Stars be with us all," Keifar nodded, addressing the group one final time. "MOVE OUT!"

Grass, dirt, and rock exploded upward as all manner of weaponry tore through the world around them. The once pristine clearing now lay in ruin, covered in smouldering craters as all about fires burned away the once plush green grass. The air was filled with smoke, an ever darkening fog of war. Like countless soldiers before them, the group of volunteers charged into the unknown; the full force of hell met with them. Surrounding Keifar in a defensive circle they moved with pace off the exit ramp. Within mere seconds three were already dead, struck down before they even had a chance to return fire. Blood erupted from their wounds, Keifar covered with the arterial spray of a man whom mere seconds ago had sworn to protect him. He had no time to check if they were OK but his heart told him they were dead and he trusted his heart. The cacophony of laser fire was deafening, audibly worsened by the sheer volume of aerial bombardment and the engines of the two battle cruisers overhead. This was a battle unlike any these men had borne witness to, the Corporal included, and the ferocity of war noticeably shook even the most stalwart of their group.

"STEADY," the General yelled as the group moved forward toward a mound of dirt, "steel yourselves!" Meanwhile Havoc had launched himself skyward, switching from bi-pedal mode near instantaneously. Weaving in and out of aerial fire like a leaf on the wind, amongst the multitude of threats that currently called the sky their home, he frantically took video of the ground below.

"Sir!" he called out over the comm, "Blackjacks incoming, due south of your position."

"SHIT!" Keifar exclaimed as the group dived to the ground behind the mound. He withdrew his holo-comm from a pouch on his vest and switched to Havoc's view. There, a faint red outline identifying them as targets, three Blackjacks advanced amongst the front line of marines. "Motherfucker, we've got Blackjacks," Keifar lamented. "Never easy, why is war never easy."

At the Corporal's command several of the volunteers opened up suppressive fire on the advancing line of enemy combatants whilst the designated heavy support set up the Ground to Air pods. "Corporal," Keifar yelled. "We have a problem." Before the Corporal could respond Havoc interrupted, his tone noticeably stalwart.

"It's been a pleasure, sir," he announced, "thank you for knocking me out all those weeks ago!"

Keifar immediately looked to the skies, fearing the drone was about to be struck. That was far from the truth. Havoc flew at pace towards the frontline of the enemy, peppered by enemy fire as he did so. Despite hit after hit he continued on his trajectory without deviation. Keifar watched on from afar as the former journalist switched to bi-pedal mode nearly five hundred feet up as he reached terminal velocity. "What's he doing?" the Corporal exclaimed, frantically trying to assist in the set-up of a Ground to Air pod after its owner fell to a grenade.

"Havoc you son of a bitch," Keifar smirked, "he's buying us time is what he is doing."

"How?" the Corporal exclaimed, occasionally letting off a burst of fire from his pistol as he fiddled with the launcher at his feet.

"By becoming a thermonuclear bomb," Keifar continued.

A bright flash illuminated the battlefield, overpowering the daylight for the briefest of moments and forcing the unit to bury their heads lest they be blinded. Seconds later a near deafening explosion rocked the world around them. It left a ringing in their ears. Shortly afterward a huge wave of air, carrying all manner of dirt, debris and charred remains washed over the mound. "This is our window team," Keifar yelled. "Make it count."

"LAUNCH!" the Corporal yelled, pulling the activation cable on his own pod. In quick succession the six Ground to Air pods exploded upward, their ordinance launched into the skies above. As designed, the main pod reached an altitude of one thousand feet before bursting into eight smaller pods, each launching off in a separate direction. On the ground, confident that they had done what they could, the remaining volunteers opened fire on the remnant of the enemy line. As planned, the skies above them were momentarily cleared as the Ground to Air pods worked their magic, chasing down each and every Variable Altitude Raider they could find. "Romero, come in, over," Keifar called out across the comm.

"This is Romero, over," he responded immediately.

"Launch!" Keifar yelled as he opened fire on the advancing soldiers. He knew he didn't need to ask again!

***

Mahira grabbed 'Ikle Paulie' so tight that all the stuffing went to his head. Romero frantically darted his hands across the control panel and then momentarily he paused. He noticed the little girl was on edge. "We'll be OK," he pledged, laying a hand upon her shoulder and softly clinching, his eyes meeting hers, "I made a promise that I intend to keep."

"I'm scared," she exclaimed, her eyes watering as her skin flushed red with worry. Romero bit down on his bottom lip, and briefly turned away. He'd never had a child of his own, nor had there been any children in his immediate family. Now he had accepted the responsibility of helping care for one, promising Keifar that if it came to the worst he would get Mahira to safety. Romero had done so not just because he cared for the safety of the young girl, but because the Montiz family had already lost so much to this war he felt they needn't lose any more.

"I know you're scared, do you want to know a secret?" Romero responded, leaning in close and smiling. "Everyone is scared, but we're tough aren't we?"

"Mmh Hmm," Mahira replied with a subtle nod. "Then we'll both be just fine," he finished.

"Romero, come in, over," the comm reverberated with Keifar's voice.

"This is Romero, over," he replied almost immediately, his hands returning to finalising the pre-flight checks. He knew what was coming.

"Launch!" Keifar yelled, the sounds of incoming fire reverberating throughout the cockpit. Mahira noticeably cowered in her chair. Romero didn't have time to console her, their window of opportunity wasn't big enough.

The hanger doors burst outward, revealing the hanger below. Romero had triggered the emergency release to give them the element of surprise. It worked. Above the hanger, enemy combatants scouting the area suddenly found themselves flung in all directions. Those lucky enough to avoid the blast leapt for cover, hiding from the explosive doors. The rest were battered, broken, and flung like rag dolls into the dirt. Before the survivors could react the skimmer burst into the air, turning ninety degrees toward its destination as it did so. Confident in escape Romero triggered the forward thrust. The skimmer didn't move. "Shit!" he exclaimed, frantically trying to ascertain why it wasn't moving. Instinctively he peered out the cockpit window, his heart sank. On the ground, shimmering like the day it was built, a single Blackjack looked upward, a sky anchor in its arms. The sky anchor, unwieldy to the common trooper, was a near archaic weapon designed to stop VTOL launches. Romero now found himself on the unfortunate end of one. Beside the Blackjack the assisting troops started to regain their footing and ready their weapons. In a flash Romero grabbed Mahira and held her tightly, he feared the worst.

***

Dr Maronne had never run so fast in her life, let alone under duress and having sustained life threatening injuries a mere day before, but the entire plan depended on it. All around her soldiers and civilians frantically prepared for evacuation, loading onto six-wheelers in their droves whilst others fled into the access tunnels and sewers. *'Three Sixteen'* was in full swing, but the most important objective was in danger of failing. Not if she could help it.

Smashing through the armoury door she yelled to the marine packing the essentials, "Fusion rifle! We have one right? Please tell me we still have one."

"Yes ma'am, I just packed it over there," he responded, gesturing to the huge crate in the corner,

"Why do you ask?"

"Because I need it!" she exclaimed moving towards it with haste, like her own life depended on it.

"Ma'am it takes two people to use it and we don't have time to set up the tripod!" the marine exclaimed with genuine concern.

"Then it's your lucky day marine, you're coming with me!" she smiled, grabbing the rifle out of the box and motioning for him to collect the power core.

Bursting out through the access hatch above the hanger, without due care for stealth, Dr Maronne and her newly acquired subordinate appeared. As they did so the shuttle burst out the hanger and into a hover, executing a ninety degree turn. All about them enemy soldiers lay prone but the one causing the most trouble, the Blackjack, caught the shuttle with its sky anchor.

"No time to set up, marine!" Dr Maronne yelled. "This is gonna hurt."

She dropped to a knee, bracing the huge fusion rifle across her thigh. The sheer weight of it was almost too much to bear on its own and that was before firing. Pure determination wiped all fear and doubt from her mind, she didn't care for the challenge or the risks. At this point Mahira was what mattered, the main objective, and she was in that shuttle. Severely flustered yet equally determined, the marine connected the power core and braced himself against Dr Maronne in a blind attempt to minimise kick back. "I should say something witty," she spat. "But I'm too *pissed*!"

The beam of pure energy burst forth from the weapon with such ferocity that Dr Maronne didn't have time to fully brace herself. Anchored to his own spot, the Blackjack had nowhere to go as its entire torso simultaneously exploded out its back and melted under the sheer heat of the directed beam. Dr Maronne managed to hold it just long enough to get the hit she needed before she was thrown near ten feet backward. She hit the ground in a heap, her clavicle giving way under the force of the landing. The pain shot through her like lava from an erupting volcano and yet despite the intense agony, she had a smile on her face.

Hearing the ruckus, Romero released Mahira and looked out the window. Beneath him the smouldering wreck of the Blackjack dropped to its knees before collapsing in a heap on the floor. The ace pilot didn't stop to think. Frantically hitting the activation button he grabbed the stick and hit the throttle. "Here we go kiddo, told you we'd get out of there!" he exclaimed with joy, dropping down below the tree line,

"No you didn't," Mahira responded, fully aware that he had instead grabbed hold of her to shield her from an attack that never came.

"Well," Romero replied, "I should have!"

"Romero, this is Dr Maronne, over," a familiar voice came over the comm, noticeably unhinged by pain.

"Maronne are you OK?" he questioned,

"I am fine, I just wanted to tell Mahira to look after Keifar for me…he can't look after himself," she responded with jest. Mahira chuckled. Before the little girl could respond however the communication was cut and she looked to Romero, tears swelling in her eyes. Keeping one eye on his flight path, he placed his hand on Mahira's shoulder and smiled.

"Dr Maronne is a tough lady, she'll be fine," he assured, his words brimming with honesty. In the back of his mind he could not help but fear the worst and yet at the same time, his gut told him if anyone could survive it would be Dr Maronne.

***

"Corporal, we gotta move, it's time," Keifar yelled, tapping him on the shoulder as he returned fire toward the oncoming soldiers. Havoc's distraction had bought them time, and allowed them to clear the skies, but the ground assault had returned with force.

"This isn't going to be pretty!" the Corporal grunted, looking toward the tree line. There was approximately four hundred yards between the mound and the trees, with no cover in between. Together the pair of them stared at the monumental task and simultaneously laughed.

"Five men left. No cover. Under heavy fire…" the Corporal continued. "I always did like a challenge sir! Stay low, we'll get you there."

With that the Corporal moved to the edge of the mound to take a peek. As he peered out a chunk of the dirt was blown back into his face, shredding skin as it went and leaving a nasty cut that began to pour blood. Had his reactions not been on par he would have lost an eye, but that didn't faze him. Turning back to the remaining volunteers he spat out the mud from his mouth and wiped the blood from his brow.

"Men, it's time to take the General home!" he commanded to the last four volunteers. Keifar was moved by the loyalty he had been shown today, the determination of his men and women warmed his heart. In those moments, he knew he could never let them down. Slapping him across the shoulder the Corporal brought Keifar hurtling back to the present, "General. Stay low. LET'S MOVE!!!"

If emerging from the exit ramp was hell, this was something far darker. No sooner had they broke from the safety of the cover they lost a man. The rookie, a kid barely out of his teens, took a laser round straight threw the eye. The back of his head disintegrated as it exploded outward with the force of the blast, spraying the group with blood, bone and brain matter. One shard of bone connected with the Corporal's cheek, piercing through to the inside of his mouth. Still he didn't flinch, he had one goal in mind. Dropping to a knee another of the other volunteers yelled for them to continue forward before unreservedly opening fire on the enemy. Shot after shot peppered his torso and still he did not relent until his last breath, his finger tight on the trigger until the very end.

Keifar's breathing hastened as he tried to maintain a sprinters pace, keeping low and ignoring the hail of laser fire all around him. The Corporal sprinted beside him, placing himself in the line of fire in case the worst should happen. He took multiple hits to the arm and the leg, but like a machine his adrenalin and sheer determination kept him moving forward. They had covered two hundred yards before another volunteer dropped, a single precise shot piercing through her lower abdomen and instantly paralysing her from the waist down. Despite the life ending injury she continued to lay down covering fire from a prone position, valiantly fighting on until a sniper finally picked her off. The tree line grew closer and closer. "Incoming!!!" the last remaining volunteer yelled, striking fear into their hearts. A grenade, the size of a baseball, landed and bounced toward Keifar's feet. Time began to slow, Keifar and the Corporal were moving at such a pace that they could not deviate. Both of them closed their eyes and braced for impact, the sounds of conflict becoming distant and distorted. Yet seconds later they were still moving forward. Behind them last volunteer had made the ultimate sacrifice, throwing himself on the grenade to absorb the brunt of the explosion. Keifar and the Corporal kept running as a crimson haze of bone and shrapnel filled the air behind them. Bits pierced their armour, scoring minor wounds, but they were still alive and moving. As the tree line drew within reach Keifar began to roar with feral determination, drawing out every ounce of strength he had left. He wasn't going to die today.

Both of them dived into the tree line without a care for how they would land. Laser fire, shrapnel and explosives tore into the trees behind them but they were clear, they made it.

Keifar was shaking off the effects of his adrenaline and the tendrils of shock that nipped at his psyche when he realised all was not well. Behind him the Corporal dropped to a knee, clutching his abdomen. Blood poured from an open wound. His breathing was staggered, his strength waning as the adrenaline ceased being enough to keep him going. "Get to the ship General," he spat, blood pooling around his gums. "I'll cover you!"

"I'll get you there, we can use the first aid kit!" Keifar responded with genuine empathy, darting back toward the Corporal.

In a sign of defiance the Corporal raised his gun toward Keifar and forced a smile. "I'll cover you!" he reiterated, before resting himself against the nearest tree, checking his rifle as he did so. Keifar knew that if it wasn't for the sacrifice of his volunteers he wouldn't have made it but he had hoped some might survive.

After everything the Corporal had been through this wasn't how he'd hoped the loyal soldier would go out. "I'll come back for you!" Keifar commanded, "Maybe not tomorrow, maybe not next week, or next month, but I will come back for you, all of you."

"I…don't doubt that sir," the Corporal smiled. "Make sure I have a metal memorial plate…pretend I said something heroic with my last breath."

Keifar smiled, "Wouldn't have it any other way."

***

Romero pulled the shuttle low to the ground, initiated a hover and then unbuckled his restraints. Drawing his sidearm, he kneeled in the hatchway and struck the door release. The hiss of hydraulics signalled its opening and the cool air from outside saturated the cargo compartment. Outside, the forest was eerily silent but for the distant sounds of battle. Romero was immediately put on edge. It was too quiet and it filled him with a sense of foreboding he truly didn't need. After everything that had occurred Romero refused to trust to fate and thus here he was, armed and ready for a fight. "Mahira keep your head down OK!" he shouted into the cockpit. "Uncle Keifar will be here soon."

"Sooner than soon," a familiar voice piped up from behind a tree, his voice broken, breathing staggered. "Let's get out of…"

Before Keifar could finish speaking the fear inducing sound of an electrical charge rang through the air and he collapsed to the ground.

"No!" Romero yelled out, looking around to see where the Blackjack was. Another shot rang out soon after, eating up dirt near Keifar's position. Mahira began screaming from the cockpit as Romero now found himself torn between the girl he had sworn to protect and the General he had promised to evacuate. With an all too familiar sound of metal on dirt, the Blackjack picked up pace, its weighed foot falls drawing closer. Romero tensed, quickly checking the clip on his pistol and cocking the chamber. Taking a deep breath in and placing his hand on the door release, ready to close it behind him, he was about to move. Then came the sound of laser fire. Breaking the eerie silence that had once more befallen the forest the crackling of electronics and searing of metal followed.

By this point Romero's breathing was heightened as Mahira's wailing from the cockpit kept him from checking on Keifar. "Fuck," a familiar voice yelled out. "You better not be dead you bastard!"

"Cass?" Romero yelled. "What?"

"No time to explain flyboy, grab the med kit! Stars be damned if I lose the son of a bitch now," she commanded, sprinting across and skidding to her knees beside the downed General.

"I'm OK," Keifar responded immediately, much to Cass' surprise.

Keifar was in one piece, not a scratch on him just the remnant of his trousers smouldering away with the leaves around him. "Sixty eight point seven two percent machine," he smirked, recalling the conversation with his brother, "turns out titanium is good protection against railgun fire."

"You lucky bastard!" Cass replied, slapping him on the back. "By the stars I thought you were dead!"

Keifar stared at her in disbelief, unsure whether to accept her concern for his safety. She looked at him and realised as much, standing to her feet and resuming her cold demeanour. "I had been tracking a group of four Blackjacks near here, they left New

Arsia two hours ago so I knew something was afoot," she continued, "but I didn't think the OPA would make a move this big."

"Well they did but Maronne has it under control," Keifar responded, marching towards the shuttle where Romero waited eagerly, "get back to what you were doing Cass."

Cass looked at him intently and she knew he was hiding something. "You've got no one left to cover you have you?" she surmised, reloading her rifle as she did so and checking the power read out.

"What's it to you?" Romero interjected. "He's got me, that's all he needs."

"No offence fly boy, but in a firefight I'd rather have me than you," Cass retorted, moving towards the shuttle.

Keifar threw his rifle onto the shuttle and then turned towards her in time to put a hand to her chest. "You're not coming with me," he grunted, his eyes still filled with the distrust she had brought down upon them all. Before Cass could react the group were silenced by a small voice.

"Cass?" Mahira whimpered. "Is that you Aunty Cass?" In that instant Cass' heart melted and her expression soon followed with it.

"Mahira?" she responded, reaching out in anticipation of a hug. The little girl sprinted from the cockpit, leapt clean past Romero to land in Cass' arms.

"Is she coming with us Uncle Keifar???" Mahira asked in jubilation, the first time she had been excited since her father past.

"That she is," he responded, feigning a smile and laying a welcoming, yet tight, hand upon Cass' shoulder. As Mahira disappeared back into the shuttle Keifar's eyes narrowed once more and his expression darkened. "One wrong move," he whispered, "I'll kill you myself."

Chapter Fourteen

The skimmer dropped into hover just outside the designated co-ordinates. Romero was all but certain this was where the access to the underground complex was, but spotting it from where they were would be difficult. Further still he couldn't risk breaking the tree line for fear of alerting the battlecruisers in high atmosphere, or they'd be gone before they even had a chance to look. "This is as far as I can take us," Romero said, turning to face Keifar beside him, Mahira perched upon his lap. "If I try to get some height to look for the access tunnel, we'll be smoke before we knew it."

"This will be fine," Keifar smiled and nodded, "let's set her down and get moving."

"I'm not coming," Romero continued, his tone suggesting he had other ideas, "I'm going back, for Maronne and the others, I owe it to them, to you." Keifar had hoped his loyal friend would continue on with him but part of him always felt Romero's place would be here on Hakon IV.

"I can't say I'm not disappointed," Keifar said, laying a welcome hand upon his friends shoulder, "but I'm not surprised, they'll need people like you."

"Not to mention nobody else can fly like you do," Cass interjected popping her head into the cockpit. Romero looked at her in astonishment. "Don't look so surprised, I can compliment," she continued.

Romero just stared at her with a troubled mix of respect and vehement distaste, his eyes narrowed and his brow lowered. To everyone's surprise Mahira jumped up onto the pilot's chair and embraced him, forcing Romero's expression to change almost instantly. In that briefest of moments he didn't know how to react, eventually accepting that he should put his arm around her. "Thank you," she whispered, "for helping protect me."

"Anytime kiddo," he replied with a smile. Keifar looked on, a smile across his own lips. Despite the knowledge that it would be just him and Cass from this point on, he was content in the knowledge that Romero could do good work here.

Cass dragged Keifar's military backpack off the skimmer and heaved it up onto her shoulders, causing Mahira to look at her and clap. "Uncle Keifar's bag is big," she said with childish glee, "you are strong aunty Cass."

"A strong, independent, woman," Cass smiled, "just like you will be one day little princess."

"No I won't," Mahira protested, folding her arms, "princesses don't carry bags."

"Yes Cass, surely that is Princess 101." Keifar interrupted, leaping down from the skimmer doorway, grabbing his rifle as he did so.

"I wouldn't know, I never was a princess," she smirked in response, slightly sticking her tongue out, "apart from my prom, or was that you?"

Keifar frowned. As Cass and Mahira ganged up on him it reminded him of how Nishfar used to do the same when they were young. "We need to find this door," he continued, turning their attention back to the task at hand. Here, the forest was thicker and greener than most, barely explored since the first colonisation efforts many decades ago. Finding the entrance to the underground complex would be difficult regardless of terrain, the dense foliage only exacerbated the already troublesome situation. Romero grabbed the side hatch and turned towards the group, his attention fixed firmly on Keifar.

"I'll be seeing you, General," Romero saluted with proud countenance, "may the Stars be with you…son."

His final words brought a contented smile to Keifar's expression. As the side-hatch closed, the hiss of hydraulics and the click of the locking mechanism signalling it was secured, Keifar saluted his comrade one last time. With Mahira and Cass at his side he took a step back. As the skimmer made a quick, sharp, one hundred and eighty degree turn, the three of them waved farewell. With a sharp burst of wind, raising all manner of loose foliage into the air, the skimmer shot forward into the dense forest beyond.

"May the Stars guide you, flyboy!" Cass whispered as she gave one final salute. "That's our cue."

Before Keifar could respond Mahira began marching off into the dense forest. Both he and Cass shared a delighted expression neither had experienced in a good few months, it was the warmth neither would forget anytime soon.

With every footstep Mahira seemed to uncover more and more bugs, something she clearly abhorred. Keifar tried his hardest to avoid the densest paths, to make it easier on his niece, yet the world around them was so overgrown that it was a far greater challenge than he had expected. Both him and Cass had their rifles at the ready, loaded but with the safeties on. Whilst Keifar was focused on Mahira and the path ahead, Cass' eyes remained fixed firmly on the rainforest around them. The sounds of wildlife muted the now distant sounds of conflict which helped keep Mahira calm, but it was still too close for comfort. Mahira had awarded 'Ikle Paulie' a battlefield promotion to smile manager, after the events of the skimmer, and he was under her command. Both Cass and Keifar played along, seeing it as the perfect distraction for a little girl changed by the shadow of war. As they continued marching forwards something close by caught Cass' attention. "Stop!" she called out, her voice lowered and her stance lowering with it. Without pause Keifar moved up to his niece, pulled her close and crouched. Mahira began to shake.

Silence befell the group. Cass reverted to military sign language to notify Keifar of what she had seen, gesturing toward a space roughly three hundred yards due south of them. In amongst the trees, carrying a large assortment of bags and furniture, walked a family of five. Two small boys, not much older than Mahira by Keifar's estimations, led the contingent shortly followed by what they presumed were the mother, father and grandfather. Usually this would have been of little concern, after all they were no doubt other refugees, but Cass paid particular notice to the father; he was armed. Gesturing to Keifar to identify the potential threat, she alerted him to the gun and estimations of the man's weight, size and potential reaction speed. Keifar cleared away some of the bushes beside him, creating a hollow for Mahira to sit in. "Stay low, stay quiet," he whispered, placing a subtle kiss upon her forehead.

"We'll be right back," Cass followed up, putting Keifar's pack down beside Mahira, "your job is to protect this."

Mahira nodded, clutching 'Ikle-Paulie' tightly in her arms. "We've got this," she whispered, giving way to a subtle, warming smile.

Keifar emerged from the forest with his arms held high. He'd left his rifle on the ground six yards back, tucking his side arm into his trousers and concealing it under his jacket. He moved slowly so as not to scare the young boys at the front and immediately the father trained his rifle on him. "*Para para!*" the man yelled, "*Para para!*"

"No harm, I mean you know harm," Keifar exclaimed, lightly gesturing to reveal he wasn't armed, "I just want to ask a question."

"*O que ele disse?*" the man questioned, turning to his wife for answers. She shrugged and looked to the taller of her young boys. "*O que ele disse?*" she reiterated.

"*Ele diz que não quer nos machucar,*" the young boy replied, pointing towards Keifar and smiling. The father, gun still trained on Keifar, summoned his son toward him and then lowered himself to his height. Keifar couldn't hear what they were saying, but even if he could he didn't speak what he presumed to be Old Portuguese. Keifar could feel sweat forming on his brow as the man with the gun trained on him betrayed nothing with his expression. Breaking the tense atmosphere the boy took a step toward Keifar and smiled, "My dad says leave, he does not want to hurt you either." The boy's countenance portrayed a child far beyond his years and he lowered his expression, a genuine sadness crossing his lips, "I'm sorry."

"*Desculpa, desculpa,*" the father continued, "*vá, vá.*"

"Drop it!" Cass yelled. Keifar sighed, having lost the chance to try and defuse the situation. Almost immediately the mother let off a howling scream that ended only once the grandfather had stood in front of her. The fathers expression immediately dropped, his eyes speaking a thousand words where his voice could say none. "*Largue,*" Cass continued, moving closer as she did so. Resigned to defeat, the father slowly placed the crude rifle on the floor and kicked it towards Keifar. "Cass, lower your weapon!" Keifar ordered, a clear and noticeable distaste in his tone as he reached down to pick up the father's gun. Cass looked at him in surprise, not willing to let her aim drop. She didn't trust anyone, especially those who didn't speak universal standards of *'Old English'* or *'Neo Mandarin'*.

Keifar looked at her sternly, the corner of his lip twitching with distaste. "Lower your weapon," he continued, this time with a tone so flammable it could ignite his rage. Not wishing to push him any further than she had to, especially near Mahira, she begrudgingly did so.

"Tell your father, I'm sorry, we seek only to know where you are going and if we can go too. Tell him I will give him back his gun," Keifar continued, looking to the young boy to translate for him. The young boy was clearly put at ease thanks to Keifar's demeanour. He turned to his father with a smile and moved to whisper in his ear. The pair conversed for a couple of minutes that seemed to last an eternity. The father's eyes never leaving Keifar's. Still suspicious and untrusting, Cass kept her finger on the trigger and the safety off. Her rifle was lowered to one side so as not to draw attention to that fact, from Keifar as much as the group around him. Eventually the boy turned back to Keifar with a smile on his lips and an obvious air of excitement.

"He says that you can walk with us," the boy said, "we are going to the lifeboats."

"Lifeboats?" Keifar asked, he had already surmised they meant the contingency ships but he needed to be sure.

"Yes sir," the boy responded, "they'll take us away from this war!"

"Sim?" the father asked in his native tongue, a word Keifar knew.

"Sim!" he responded, handing the father back his gun.

"Mahira!" Cass yelled into the forest, seconds later the little girl came trundling out of the foliage, feebly attempting to drag her uncles bag. Noticing her struggle Cass moved over and grabbed the gear, easily raising it up and on to her shoulders as she grabbed Keifar's rifle off the ground. "Mahira this is… I'm sorry, what were your names?"

"I am Anselmo," the boy answered with a smile, "my younger brother is Calisto, my father is Gaspar, my mother Luísa and my grandfather, Modesto."

"It's a pleasure to meet you all," Keifar responded, the boy quick to translate for him. "I am Keifar, my over protective associate there is Cass and this is my niece, Mahira." Overcome with a sudden blushing shyness, Mahira took cover behind her uncle's leg and he could not help but chuckle. "She isn't usually this shy," he smiled, trying to wrestle her free from his leg, "usually."

With their new found assistance it took less than an hour for them to find the entrance to the underground. Keifar had agreed to take some of the weight off the old man's shoulders, as a gesture of goodwill, and Cass took point so as not to antagonise those around her. Meanwhile Mahira had slowly warmed to the presence of Calisto and Anselmo, eventually enjoying the company of children her own age. For Keifar it was a joy to behold. Much to Cass' suspicion, Gaspar had stayed silent for the entire journey, not even speaking to his wife or the grandfather. Furthermore he never took his eyes of Cass, something that had not escaped the experienced marine's notice. Keifar would also have considered his silence suspicious but he was distracted by the improvement to Mahira's mood. Cass lamented the fact he was so easily blinded yet she could not blame him. It further signalled why he needed her along for the ride. "*Como abrimos isso?*" Gaspar announced, breaking his hour long silence as he felt around the edges of the two meter wide door frame. By colony standards it was archaic in design and bore no resemblance to any military compound or facility Keifar had ever been too.

"My dad asks how do we open this?" Anselmo piped up.

"That, Anselmo, is a good question," Keifar responded, first looking to the boy and then his father before returning his attention to the door. "Cass, any ideas?"

"We blow it open," she answered forcefully, marching past Keifar with a thermite charge, "old fashioned yet reliable, get everyone to cover."

"*Explosão, esconder,*" Anselmo commanded, yelling at his family with surprising authority. No sooner had the young boy mentioned explosives did his family move with startling haste. Keifar and Mahira fell into step with them. Taking cover behind a four meter wide tree that stood taller and thicker than those around it, the group huddled closely. Seconds later Cass came barrelling around the tree and slammed her back to it, her breathing staggered. "*Fogo no buraco!*" she yelled, a smile emblazoned across her face. Keifar and Mahira looked at her with confusion, but as soon as the others raised their hands to their ears they followed suit.

The explosion was brief but loud. Almost instantly flocks of birds, small and large, burst from the trees above. Vast in number, their fluttering was almost as loud as the explosion. Cass peered her head out from behind the tree and smirked. Where once the outcropping and the double door had stood, now lay a crater leading into a barely lit tunnel. She recognised that she may have over done it but right now it didn't really bother her. "I'm quite proud of my work," she exclaimed turning to face the family; then fear took hold and instinct took over. She raised her rifle and aimed it straight at Gaspar as he stood over the unconscious body of Keifar, his own gun pointed to Mahira's head. The little girl was sobbing, frozen in the spot, 'Ikle-Paulie' nowhere to be seen.

She looked to Anselmo and Calisto for help but they just shied away, trying in vain to hide their own tears. "Drop your weapon!" Anselmo commanded, looking directly at Cass, "or my father will shoot Mahira!"

"Tell your father I can't do that," Cass replied through gritted teeth, her eyes fixed on him with a venom few survived, "he should understand."

"*Ela não pode fazer isso*," Anselmo exclaimed, turning to face his father. Cass took the chance his moment of distraction gave her. Laser fire echoed out through the rainforest. Gaspar's head exploded in a shower of grey matter, blood and bone. Anselmo and his remaining family froze in abstract shock and horror. "What your father did not realise," Cass growled, her eyes still over flowing with rage, "is that I am not one of the good people!"

Mahira's eyes stayed closed, her sobs muted against the heavy footfalls of the family as they hastily retreated in fear. "Mahira," Cass whispered, her rifle firmly fixed on those that fled. "Are you OK?"

"Did you mean that?" the little girl exclaimed through snot and tears, "did you mean you're not one of the good people."

"Of course not," Cass replied, her tone calm in an attempt to sooth the little girl's fears, "but they were going to hurt you I had to scare them to make sure they didn't." Despite the words spoken Cass appreciated she was straying far from the truth. She knew she wasn't one of the good ones because in war you never truly can be. She had accepted that the day she agreed to kill Keifar.

"What on this...planet?" Keifar grumbled, emerging from his force induced unconsciousness. His eyes met Gaspar's body on the ground beside him and he let off a forlorn sigh, burying his head in his hands. Like he had said to his brother, war changes people.

"We need to move, Keifar," Cass shouted, "if anyone else is around this won't have gone unnoticed."

"That and time is not on our side, they could launch that shuttle any moment," Keifar responded, pulling himself to his feet. Mahira had yet to stop sobbing and so he took her in his arms, lifting her off the ground has he did so. "Hey," he whispered, his tone soft in an attempt to comfort her, "don't be sad, Aunty Cass saved us."

"I know," she sobbed, gripping the reunited 'Ikle Paulie' tightly, "I'm sad because I made a friend and then he was mean to us." Keifar could not help but bite his bottom lip and furrow his brow, trying hard to hold off the mixture of sorrow and anger with which he wanted to respond. He knew now that he never should have trusted them in the first place, but he couldn't let Mahira know that or she would never trust again.

"Let's go," Cass commanded, confident that the family was out of range, "the sooner we leave this place, the better."

Chapter Fifteen

The tunnel was damp, barely lit and carried a breeze that sent everyone's hairs standing on end. A faint buzz of electricity skirted along the edges of the walls, contained within rusty iron pipes that held a flickering halogen lightbulb every six meters. For Keifar and Cass it was like walking into the history books, for Mahira it was another adventure and a distraction from the trauma she experienced mere moments ago. Cass stayed no more than two or three strides ahead of the others, careful to watch her footing as she went. Both her and Keifar had experienced similar in the tunnels under New Arsia but these tunnels were older, quieter and far cooler than those. Further still they seemed longer. It took them half an hour moving forward before they reached an intersection with two doors. "I sure hope Romero was right," Cass piped up, breaking the silence.

"Our scouts never got it wrong before, doubt they would now," Keifar responded, his tone conveying obvious distaste at the suggestion the intel wasn't good, "and Romero was always one to double check."

"Very well," Cass replied, turning to face him, "left or right?"

"Right!" Keifar answered self-assuredly.

"How can you be sure?" Cass continued, knowing full well his intel didn't include such specific directions.

"Because that is the direction the pipes go in and they have to be getting their power from somewhere," Keifar responded with a smirk.

Cass looked to the pipes and then back at him with an eyebrow raised, "You have a valid point."

A further ten minutes passed as they journeyed down the right hand tunnel. Mahira had fallen asleep in Keifar's arms, forcing him to carry his rifle in one hand. He hoped he wouldn't need to use it anytime soon but considering this war had a habit of surprising him it remained in his hand.

"We have to entertain the idea that it may have been wrong," Cass said, breaking the silence, deference in her tone. "I don't mean to be a sour apple, but you know better than anyone that you should plan for the worst."

"And be pleasantly surprised by the best...not this time," he exclaimed, a passion in his voice she had seldom experienced of late. Her head dropped for a second and she stopped in her tracks, forcing Keifar to pause as well.

"I want this to be true as much as you," she said, looking directly towards him, "but I also want you to know that if it isn't I will do everything to get you and that little girl of this planet." Keifar gave an even-tempered nod, wishing not to respond for fear of masquerading an insult as a compliment. He still had not forgiven Cass for what had happened, nor did he believe he ever would, yet where others would have fled she had stayed to help. It was a loyalty he would never have expected from someone who mere days ago was seeking to assassinate him.

Without warning a stentorian rumble shook them from their discussion, shaking the tunnel walls and raining dust down upon the three. Mahira woke up with shock, instinctively gripping Keifar by the scruff of the neck and burying her head into his chest. Cass' eyes darted around, frantically trying to find cover where there was none. She feared a cave in could put an end to their journey and stars be damned if she was going to let that happen now. Seconds after the rumble began, a large gust of air swept through the tunnel carrying with it an unnerving warmth that was almost too hot to bear. Keifar froze.

Cass looked at him and both of them instinctively knew what the other was thinking. "RUN!" she yelled. Immediately they turned on their heels and made haste toward the hatch they had just come through. Keifar's speed was phenomenal, thanks to his cybernetic legs, but Cass on the other hand struggled to keep up.

"Drop the bag!" Keifar yelled,

"But the supplies, the food, water!" Cass exclaimed, struggling more and more to keep up.

"No use to us if we're dead!" Keifar called back. "Drop it!!!"

Cass didn't care to answer or contest, she was happy to be done with it. Without a moment's pause she withdrew her knife and cut through the shoulder straps. The bag dropped in a heap on the ground and immediately her pace improved. She was nowhere near as fast as Keifar but she was fast enough. Turning to look over her shoulder, Cass could see the feint orange light of an inferno gathering in the distance. "We're running out of time! Keifar" she exclaimed, obvious worry in her tone.

"I can see the hatch!" he yelled,

"I can see the fire!!!" Cass replied with clear apprehension, the tension was on the rise and the fear was palpable. They had very little time.

Keifar burst through the hatch, tripping over the lip and falling to the ground. Luckily he was able to twist just in time to take the brunt of it on his back and protect Mahira from being crushed. Seconds later Cass came barrelling through. "FUUUUUUUUCK!!!" she yelled as she slammed her hand on the door controls. As the hatch closed flames bit at the edges, catching her arm and setting her top alight. Keifar leapt to his feet and began batting away the flames as Cass frantically tried to the same. "Get it off me!!!" She cried out, the flames beginning to burn the skin beneath. Withdrawing his knife, Keifar cut through the cloth at the shoulder and then tore it free, throwing it to the ground and stamping out the fire. Mahira watched on with concern that soon turned to relief. Everyone took a moment to catch their breath.

"These aren't maintenance tunnels," Keifar said, placing his hands on his knees and spitting out phlegm as he caught his breath,

"You…don't…say!" Cass responded through staggered breathing. Keifar looked at her with feigned distaste but soon forced a smile. "That had to be one of the shuttles launching, we only have one more chance," he continued, turning to face Mahira.

Her smile ignited his hope and Cass could see it immediately. "We run, down that tunnel. It's our only hope," Cass said, placing a hand on Keifar's shoulders, "you can easily make ten or fifteen miles per hour with those legs. I'll keep up as best I can, worst case you leave me behind, best case we all get on that shuttle."

Keifar looked at her for a moment, then at Mahira. "You have to hold on to me tight OK?" he asked, picking her up. "Eyes closed all the way."

"All the way," Mahira responded with a smile.

"Keifar Montiz always liked a challenge," Cass continued with a smile. "It's been a long time since he dragged me along for the ride."

Keifar's pace was blistering as he pulled every ounce of speed out of his cybernetics. With every stride there was increasing pain but he could not let that stop him, he had to make it to the shuttle before it launched. Cass did well to keep up at first but eventually she fell behind. Strangely, Keifar found himself concerned for her safety. In minutes, to his relief, he could see the end of the tunnel. It was an archway leading out into a large, brightly illuminated, open space. *That must be it,* he thought to himself, picking up the pace as best he could. He leapt into the opening, skidding to a halt in the thick layer of dust that had settled on the ground. It was at least seven hundred yards in diameter, possibly more or so Keifar estimated, and was built in the same fashion as the tunnels. Speaking of a time long before Keifar was born.

Once he had caught his breath, Keifar, followed by Mahira, slowly looked upward. They laid their eyes upon the vast hulk of the contingency shuttle and both could not help but gasp in awe. Larger in person then when they had seen it aboard the skimmer, it was a testament to the strength of human exploration and determination. "It looks like a coconut with engines," Mahira piped up breaking Keifar from his trance.

"That is one way to describe it," he responded with a smile, "now we just need to get on it."

"Not without me!" a voice called out from behind them. Cass came bounding into the room, her breathing staggered and her legs barely sustaining her weight, "It's one hell of a climb."

"You up to it?" Keifar asked, pointing towards one of the rickety ladders,

"I have to be, it's that or be cooked alive," she shrugged, attempting to catch her breath, "I'm not too keen on the latter option."

***

The group climbed the rickety ladder like their lives depended on it. They actually did. Cass had taken point climbing the ladder so as to be the first to the top and thus able to secure it. Keifar had secured Mahira to his back, using his rifle strap and she held on equally tight for extra security. It was a monumental climb yet grim determination pushed them ever forwards, the end goal within touching distance. As they drew closer to the first supporting walkway, Cass could make out a group amassing along its length. To the front of the group several men banged heavily on the side hatch, calling out for whomever was inside to open it. Cass' heart sank, if they couldn't get in when they got there then they were done for. "We might have a problem," she shouted, looking down toward Keifar and fighting back the uneasiness of vertigo, "these refugees can't get in!"

"There are multiple entry points," Keifar yelled, drawing attention to the five other walkways above the first, "maybe we can get in through one of those?"

"We're already running on borrowed time," Cass answered, "who knows when this thing will launch." As if by divine precedent, an alarm began blaring all around the launch silo.

"Three minutes to departure!" a digital voice bellowed out from the tannoy speakers dotted around, "secure all doors, finalise loading procedures."

"Shit," Keifar exclaimed, taking no care to avoid expletives in the presence of his niece, "that door is our only hope!"

Cass looked back down to him, a pensive expression over coming her worried exterior. "I've got it," she yelled. "You wait at this access point, I'll sprint ahead to the other door. Whichever one of us gets in first can then open the other door from inside."

"What if we can't?" Keifar continued, bracing himself against the ladder as they drew closer to the walk way,

"Then we're no more worse off than we are now!" Cass exclaimed, picking up the pace with her climbing.

To Keifar's amazement she began leaping from hand hold to hand hold, doubling her pace and moving her far beyond the first walkway. "Stars help us," Keifar whispered under his breath.

"It'll be OK Uncle Keifar," Mahira whispered back, "Cass will help us." In that moment, Keifar prayed to the stars his niece was right.

Cass was beginning to feel the fatigue as she drew closer to the second walkway. A steady group of people funnelled across this one and to her delight, the hatch was open. She took one last look down toward Keifar to confirm they were near the door and then braced herself. Because of its positioning direct access to the ladder wasn't possible from the second walkway and so she knew she would need to throw herself some distance. Several of the refugees caught sight of her but no one stopped to help, every single one more focused on their own survival. Although disappointed no one thought to help her, Cass couldn't blame them, like her and Keifar this was their only chance of escaping the horrors of the war. Closing her eyes and focusing, Cass took in a deep breath before using all her strength to throw herself onto the second walkway. Time stood still as she sailed through the air, arms out stretched, teeth gritted. She knew she wouldn't make the railing so she had to gamble on the edge of the grated flooring. Her hands grabbed hold with ease and she tensed her arms as her body weight took over. She could feel the muscles tear, but she was too focused to care. Many of the refugees walking above her gasped, but still no one reached down to help her up. Through sheer strength of will, Cass pulled herself up into the midst of the refugees and took a moment to catch her breath. Stood still she was buffeted from person to person as everyone frantically sought safety aboard the shuttle.

"Two minutes until launch," the digital voice bellowed from the tannoy, "secure all doors, finalise loading procedures."

"Crap, I've got to move!" Cass said to herself. "You can do this!"

Showing as much care as they had shown her, Cass barged through the crowd. Several of the refugees tried in vain to stand their ground and not let her on before themselves, but they stood little chance against the full might of Cassandra D'Cruze. When she reached the door, a single drone stood between her and the interior.

"Seat A67," it exclaimed, presenting a ticket from its abdomen, but Cass didn't stop she had to open the other door.

***

Keifar watched Cass reach the second walkway with an aura of relief. All around him the refugees were overcome with a mixture of fear and worry. Many had already resigned themselves to the idea that they weren't getting off this stars forsaken planet. But Keifar had faith Cass would get him and Mahira out of here, she had to. Pushing through the group with determination, Keifar reached the hatch and the men who were trying in vain to open it. He could see their futile attempts were beginning to take their toll as several of them had tears in their eyes and bloodied knuckles. All of their expressions were weathered by days of little sleep and malnutrition. The men and women all held a similar dejected demeanour, brightened only by the few children who were not old enough to understand the turmoil they faced. "Hold," Keifar yelled, "Hold yourselves."

"Why, what good will it do?" One of the men responded.

"We're done for!" Another piped up.

"Because you're scaring your children, think of them!" Keifar commanded, "We're all in the same situation. Banging on this hatch, wrestling with each other, resigning yourselves to a believed inevitability, none of this will help you now."

"Oh, and you will?" one of the bigger men interrupted, pushing himself to the front of the group, directly before Keifar.

"Possibly, yes!" Keifar yelled, squaring up to the man who clearly sought to intimidate him, "someone I trust with my life is going to open that hatch any minute. But believe me if you're all acting like this, she'll shoot you before you get a chance to step on that shuttle!"

The bigger man's expression darkened and he took a step closer to Keifar, yet despite the continued hostility Keifar did not flinch.

"Don't think about it," he responded with zero animosity, "especially in front of my niece."

"Leave," the man grunted, pushing Keifar backward and against the railing.

"Not until I'm on that shuttle," Keifar responded, "I'm telling you again, not in front of the children." The man's fist impacted with Keifar's jaw before he had a chance to react. He could feel a couple of his teeth pop out of place with the force of the hit, blood beginning to pool in his mouth. That would be the last hit Keifar would take. His metallic leg collided with the

179

man's shin, the sound of bone snapping making everyone cringe and causing the man to yell out in pain. As he dropped to his knee, Keifar grabbed him by the neck and raised his fist.

"STOP!" Mahira yelled out, grabbing Keifar by the leg, "Don't kill him Uncle Keifar."

Immediately he paused, releasing his grip on the man's throat and lowering his fist. He turned towards Mahira with a smile, "Thank you!"

The hiss of hydraulics and the metallic clicking of a locking mechanism signalled the hatch was opening. Inside with her rifle aimed toward the group, Cass stood proudly with a smug look on her face. "All aboard," she yelled in a mock conductor's voice, "tickets please."

"About time," Keifar smiled, walking on with Mahira by his side, "I thought you'd never show." Behind him all the refugees stood in fear, unsure how to proceed, Keifar's assailant writhing in pain on the floor.

"What happened to him?" Cass questioned, looking to Keifar for an explanation,

"A simple misunderstanding," Keifar replied without pause, "we better find some seats and get buckled up."

"Are we letting these people on?" Cass continued, gesturing with her rifle. Keifar paused for a moment and looked to Mahira. The little girl nodded without saying a word.

With a smile on his lips, Keifar turned to Cass and gave a slight nod. "Very well," she piped up. "Move your asses!"

***

The inside of the shuttle was a peculiar design. Each walkway contained a ladder for when the shuttle was in launch position and was divided by four seats. All the seats were crafted of black leather and consisted of both a waist and shoulder belt, both of which connected with a buckle in the middle. Once seated, those within would be facing towards the nose of the shuttle with their back to the ground. The decor was sparse, the metallic edges of the hull painted only in white with warning signs telling all who passed to 'watch your head'. Although clearly built for civilians it still maintained a military air about it and spoke of a time decades passed. Like the shuttles from the dawn of space travel, it jumped straight out of the history books. Keifar was in awe.

Countless men, women and children were already sat in many of the seats, many of them clenching tightly on the straps or rigorously checking and rechecking their children were secure. Climbing the laddered walkway, Keifar found him, Mahira and Cass a trio of seats near one of the windows. With glee in her eyes, Mahira leapt off Keifar's shoulder and into the seat, laying back and moving to buckle herself in. "Thirty seconds until launch," the digital voice sounded throughout the compartment, "Secure belts." With haste Keifar and Cass secured themselves, both of them quick to double check Mahira's belt was secure despite her smaller size.

Both of them breathed a collective sigh of relief, bracing themselves against their chairs and exchanging a thankful look.

The countdown began at twenty. For what seemed like an eternity, it ticked down to five and then fell silent. Keifar placed his hand in Mahira's. "Close your eyes," he whispered before resting his head back in his seat. He was right to do so. A loud rumble reverberated throughout the shuttle, shaking the seats beneath them and causing several people to scream in shock. Soon enough the whole shuttle was rattling, and Mahira gripped her uncle's hand tighter than she ever had before. Breaking the roar, a massive explosion sounded beneath them and instantly they felt the pressure of g-force rally against them.

"We're OK!" Keifar shouted, trying to comfort his niece and, in a way, himself.

"It'll be over soon!" Cass yelled in response. The little girl didn't move but she was still conscious unlike many of the other children in the shuttle. Once more the shuttle shook violently and the sound of metal upon rock broke the roar of the engines.

Keifar fought against the g-force pressing against him to look out the window. He saw the shuttle was tearing through the ground and the jungle afterward. As trees exploded outward, followed by mounds of dirt, he watched as the view cleared and he could see Hakon IV in all her glory. But she wasn't the planet he remembered. Her surface was ablaze at points and charred to a crisp at others. Smoke and ash raged across several settlements as T400 Raiders darted through the sky, raining down once forbidden ordinance. The higher the shuttle drew towards atmosphere the more scarring Keifar could see, a tear pooling in his eye. Around them several battle cruisers hastily attempted to manoeuvre into a position where they could target the shuttle, but it was too fast for them to counter. The few shots that did connect bounced off the hull with barely a shudder. Suddenly the shuttle tilted violently to the side, a stentorian screeching of metal upon metal reverberating throughout the compartment. More screams followed and Keifar looked to Cass with worry emblazoned upon his expression. "A cruiser?" Cass questioned,

"No?" Keifar responded.

Silence followed the screeching. Gravity slowly disappeared to be replaced by the weightlessness of space. Unsecured luggage and other items began floating around in the compartment, yet everyone was too afraid to unbuckle and secure them. Keifar looked out the window to see if he could see a cruiser, but there was nothing. "We're still moving forward," he said, gesturing to Cass. "Whatever it was, it didn't stop the shuttle."

"Attention!" The familiar digital voice called out through the Tannoy. "We have successfully departed Hakon IV's orbit. Our destination is… Makara III. We will arrive in…72 Earth Standard Hours."

"Makara III?" Cass questioned, looking towards Keifar.

He looked to her, and smiled, "Capital of the systems alliance…all this time I thought they were programmed for Earth. We're safe!"

"Are we still going to see Grandad?" Mahira interrupted.

"Of course," Keifar responded with glee. "We'll get another shuttle after this one and we'll see him in no time."

"Ol'Grampa Montiz," Cass said, chuckling to herself. "Never thought I'd see that old man again, always used to tease me something rotten."

"It's because he thought you fancied my brother," Keifar responded with a chuckle of his own, "how wrong he was!"

"Have you thought about your next move, after your dad?" Cass continued. "Hakon IV needs you."

"I know Cass," Keifar replied with a determined expression. "This is just beginning."

Epilogue

Eighteen Years Later

Keifar sat at the prefabricated, metallic desk with his eyes fixed firmly upon the photo of him with his brother and their father. Unlike most photos of the current age, digitalised or holographic, it was printed and framed within a rare oak. His head was resting upon his hands with fingers interlocked, and his expression appeared apprehensive at best. The years since his brother's death had not been kind to him, scars covering his battle worn visage; only partially obscured by the long, bushy, steel grey beard he had grown. In front of him lay a single, black data slate, its holographic display covered with text. He occasionally gestured at it, his eyes darting across the details before returning to look at the photo as his mind darted through a plethora of possibilities.

A short, sharp knock at the door brought his concentration to the present. "Enter!" He commanded, his deep voice as war wearied as his visage. The door, mundane in design, opened inward. A beautiful young woman, her skin soft and golden, her pearlescent jet black hair tied into a bun, entered with a trained military gait. With practiced ease she stood to attention in front of the desk, her eyes fixed firmly on the wall in front and not on Keifar. "At ease soldier." Keifar said with an unmilitary like warmth, standing from his chair as he did so. The motorised gears in his artificial legs whirled into action, a replacement long overdue. Moving around his desk, he placed his hand upon her cheek and smiled. "You're sure this is what you want?" he asked,

"Yes sir!" she responded with stern enthusiasm.

"Very well," he continued, grabbing his data slate and hitting record, "welcome to the Free Hakon Army, soldier. For the record, please identify yourself!"

The young woman smiled, "Private First Class Mahira Montiz, 1st Regiment, reporting for duty."